FRED BOWEN SPORTS STORY series

FRED BOWEN

Published by
PEACHTREE PUBLISHERS
1700 Chattahoochee Avenue
Atlanta, Georgia 30318-2112
www.peachtree-online.com

Printed and bound in July 2014 in the United States of America by RR Donnelley in Harrisonburg, Virginia
10 9 8 7 6 5 4

Library of Congress Cataloging-in-Publication Data
Bowen, Fred.
Dugout rivals / written by Fred Bowen.
p. cm.
Summary: Twelve-year-old Jake, who was one of his mediocre baseball team's best players the previous season, unexpectedly finds himself overshadowed when a new player shows up, and the team starts winning.
ISBN 978-1-56145-515-7
[1. Baseball—Fiction. 2. Competition (Psychology)—Fiction. 3. Friendship—Fiction.] I. Title.
PZ7.B6724Du 2010
[Fic]—dc22

2009024514

For my wife, Peggy Jackson,
with gratitude for all that she does

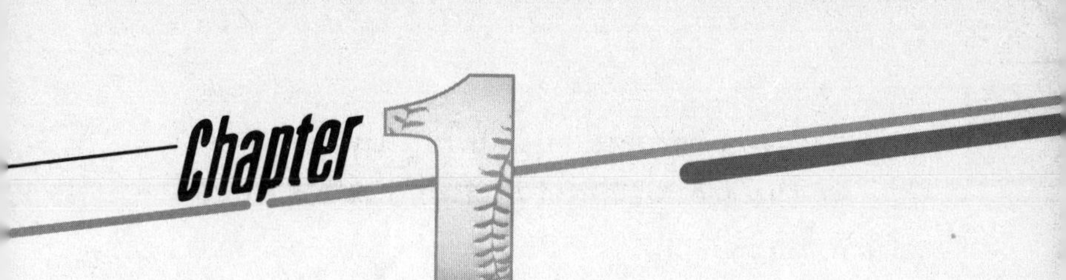

Chapter 1

Jake Daley and Ryan Duckett stood at the edge of a large field to watch dozens of players try out for the Woodside Baseball League. Jake and Ryan had brought their baseball gloves to the park even though they weren't trying out. The two friends were already on the Red Sox. They were spending this cool spring Saturday morning on the lookout for good players who might help their team.

Together they scanned the players at the four different stations: running, batting, pitching, and fielding. Jake's eyes settled on ten kids getting ready for a 30-yard dash at the running station. At the sound of the whistle, the runners took off. One boy pulled ahead quickly and flashed across the finish line two full strides ahead of the pack.

"Hey, who's that kid?" Jake asked.

Ryan had seen him too. "I don't know," he said. "But he sure is fast. He won that race easy."

Jake watched the boy pick up his glove and move to the pitching station. He was tall and slender with long arms and legs. His dark hair was tucked under a blue baseball cap.

"I think I've seen that kid around," Jake said, squinting into the sun. "He looks familiar."

Ryan shrugged. "I've never seen him."

"He might be a guy who could really help us," Jake said. "Let's go talk to him."

Jake and Ryan moved toward the line of players where the mystery kid was waiting to pitch. As Jake got closer to the line, he noticed the red *B* for Boston on the boy's baseball hat.

"Hey, nice hat!" Jake called out.

The boy turned and smiled. "Yeah, my mom's a big Red Sox fan," he said.

"My dad is too," Jake said, tapping the same red *B* on his own hat. "I'm Jake. Jake Daley." He turned and pointed his thumb at Ryan. "This is Ryan Duckett. We're both on the Red Sox. Hey, maybe you'll make our team."

"Yeah, that would be cool," the boy said as he looked at the pitching hopefuls waiting in line. "But I just want to make *a* team. I really don't care which one."

"What's your name?" asked Jake.

"Oh yeah. I'm Adam Hull."

Jake took the baseball out of his glove and held it up. "You want to warm up?" he asked Adam.

"Yeah, but I don't want to lose my place in line."

"I'll hold your spot," Ryan said.

Adam stepped out of line and jogged a few yards away from Jake. The two boys started throwing the ball back and forth, softly at first and then harder as they moved farther away from each other.

"Do you go to Whitman?" Jake asked.

"Yeah," Adam answered. "I just started last month."

"I thought I'd seen you around."

"Probably. You live on Warren Street, right?" Adam asked.

"Yeah, 17 Warren." Jake threw the ball harder.

Adam caught it easily. "My mom lives on Lewis. I've seen you on the bus in the morning. You're a couple of stops after mine." He went into his easy pitching motion and uncorked a fastball. *Sssssmack!* The ball sizzled through the air and whacked into Jake's glove.

"Watch out," Jake warned. "You don't want to throw too hard so early in the season. You'll hurt your arm."

"You mean I'll hurt *your* hand!" Adam laughed. "Don't worry, I'm not throwing that hard."

Not throwing that hard? Jake tried not to notice the stinging in his hand. Ignoring his own advice, Jake threw his hardest fastball to Adam. With a casual flick of his glove, Adam caught the ball inches from his left ear.

Wow, my best fastball didn't even faze this guy, Jake thought.

Ryan waved from the front of the pitching station line. "You'd better get over here," he called.

"Gotta go," Adam said, flipping the ball to Jake. "Thanks."

"Good luck," Jake said. "See you on the bus. Or maybe on the Red Sox."

Jake and Ryan moved to the side of the field and sat down in the cool grass. "That Adam guy looks pretty good," Ryan said.

"*Pretty good?*" Jake blurted out. "He's great. He can throw...and catch...and run...." He looked across the field. "I wonder if he can hit," he said.

"Want to bet?" Ryan laughed.

Jake definitely didn't want to bet against Adam. "Yeah, you're right. He's a player. Wouldn't it be cool if we got him for the team?"

"Yeah. With you at shortstop and a couple of new kids like Adam, we'll be a lot better than last year," Ryan said.

Jake smiled. He was twelve years old and this was his third year with the Red Sox. When he was ten, Jake had spent most of his time on the bench. At eleven, he started every game at second base. At the end of the season, the coaches had given Jake the trophy for Team's Best Eleven-Year-Old. Jake put the trophy on his dresser where he could see it every day.

Now that he was twelve, Jake was looking forward to playing shortstop every inning. He'd be the leader of the Red Sox. This year was going to be his best year ever.

"Hey, here's a couple of Red Sox," a familiar voice said from behind the boys. "How are you guys doing?"

"Hey, Coach Sanders."

The Red Sox coach pushed his hat back on his head as he surveyed the field. "You boys see anybody I should try to get for the team?"

"Yeah," Jake and Ryan blurted out together. "Adam Hull."

At the pitching area, Adam toed the rubber, went into his windup, and blistered a fastball across the center of the plate.

Coach Sanders looked down at his clipboard. "Oh yeah, I noticed him right away," he said, reviewing his notes. "Real good infielder...can field anything...terrific arm."

"He won his race, easy," Ryan added.

"Maybe he could pitch or play center field," Jake suggested. He wanted to keep shortstop for himself.

All three watched Adam whistle another pitch smack into the catcher's mitt.

"He sure looks like a great all-around player. Maybe I can figure out a way to get him on the Red Sox." Coach Sanders patted Jake on the shoulder and walked away. "See you boys next week at practice," he said with a wave.

Out on the field, Adam fired one last pitch. Another strike. Jake and Ryan exchanged grins and a quick fist bump. "We could have a *really* good team this year," Ryan said.

Jake agreed. Sitting in the soft grass and looking out over the field, he felt certain that this would be a great year, all right. This was going to be *his* year.

Chapter 2

Jake and Ryan dashed up the steps of the afternoon bus waiting at Whitman Middle School. They walked to the back amid the shouts of students and the rumble of the idling motor and grabbed their usual seats.

"I can't believe it's only Monday," Ryan complained. "I don't think I can make it through a whole week."

"Tomorrow's our first practice. That'll be cool," Jake reminded him.

"Yeah, for you," Ryan said. "Coach Sanders will put you at shortstop. He'll probably stick me in right field...or on the bench."

Jake looked up and saw a tall boy in a battered Red Sox hat board the bus and slip into a seat near the front. "Hey, there's that kid Adam," he said to Ryan. Then he called out: "Go, Red Sox!"

A kid in the middle of the bus popped up from his seat and yelled, "Red Sox stink. Go, Yankees!" The bus erupted into boos and cheers.

"Go, Red Sox!"

"Yankees rock!"

"Yankees stink!"

The bus driver, Mrs. Dedeo, stood up. "Everybody quiet down and get into your seats. We're about to go."

"Hey, Adam! Adam Hull!" Jake shouted above the noise.

Adam turned around and Jake waved.

"Come on back here," Jake called.

Adam started walking down the aisle, but not quick enough for Mrs. Dedeo. Looking into the big rearview mirror, she told him, "Get in your seat right now, young man. I'm not moving this bus until everyone is sitting down."

Adam quickly slid into the last seat with Jake and Ryan. "Man, that lady is mean," he said in a low voice.

"Don't worry about her," Jake said. "She's always in a bad mood."

He slid down the seat to make more room for Adam. "Hey, now that you're on the team," he said, "you get to sit with your teammates."

"I'm on the Red Sox?" Adam asked. "Awesome. I have to text my mom." He pulled his phone from his back pocket.

"Didn't Coach Sanders call you last night?" Ryan asked, sounding surprised.

Adam started tapping the keys on his phone. "Maybe he called my dad. I was at my mom's last night," he said, still tapping.

Jake reached into his backpack and pulled out a piece of paper. "You're definitely on the team," he said. "Here's the roster. They posted it on the league website this morning."

The boys checked out the list of names as the bus pulled away from the school.

RED SOX

Manager: Mr. Philip Sanders

Player:	Age:
Samuel Curtis	12
Jacob Daley	12
Ryan Duckett	12
Adam Hull	12
Hannah Roberts	12
Isaiah Slater	12
Khalil Williams	12
Kyle Kim	11
Alex Morales	11
Christopher Morgan	11
Michael Rios	11
Evan Sherman	11
Julian Jackson-Davis	10
Mack Radecki	10

"I don't know these kids," Adam said. "Can any of them play?"

"Sure," Jake said. "Let's see. Isaiah Slater is a really good hitter and he can pitch too. Evan Sherman can catch. Hannah's good, Sam pitches—"

"And Jake will play shortstop," Ryan interrupted.

"What was your record last year?" Adam asked.

"Five wins and nine losses."

Adam gave Jake a look that showed he wasn't very impressed.

"We lost a lot of close games," Jake added quickly. "We'll be tons better this year."

He looked out the window. The bus was getting closer to Adam's stop. "Hey, Adam, why don't you come over to my house? Ryan will be there too. We can play Wiffle ball in my backyard."

"Um, sure. Let me text my mom again."

A few minutes later, the three teammates were dashing through the Daleys' front door. "Hey, Dad, I'm home!" Jake shouted as he entered.

"I'm in my office," Mr. Daley called back. The boys dumped their backpacks on the living room floor and headed downstairs. Jake's father was at his computer, typing quickly. "I left you some chips and dip in the kitchen," he said without looking up.

"Me, Ryan, and Adam are going to play Wiffle ball in the backyard."

With that, Mr. Daley looked up from his computer and laughed. "Sorry about my bad manners. I just was finishing up an e-mail. How are you, Ryan?" Then he turned toward Adam. "I don't think we've met."

"I'm Adam."

"He lives over on Lewis," Jake said. "He's gonna be on the Red Sox this season."

"Oh, right. I saw your name on the roster this morning."

Jake looked over at Adam. "My dad's one of the assistant coaches," he said.

"I hear that you're quite a player, Adam," Mr. Daley said. "Maybe you can help the Red Sox win a few more games."

"Oh, he'll help," Ryan said. "A lot."

"Do your parents know you're here?" Mr. Daley asked as the boys started back upstairs.

"Yeah," Ryan replied.

"Yeah, my mom said it was okay," Adam said over his shoulder.

Outside in the bright afternoon sunshine, Jake explained to Adam how he and Ryan played Wiffle ball in his backyard. "A grounder that gets past both fielders is a single; a fly ball that lands past the bush is a double; anything over the fence is a home run."

"Let's hit with a regular bat," Adam suggested as he picked up a metal bat from a pile of sports equipment.

"It's a lot easier to hit with the plastic bat," Ryan said.

"That's why the metal bat is better practice," Adam said. "We won't hit with a plastic bat during the season, right?"

"Okay, we can hit with the regular bat," Jake agreed. "I'll pitch first. Adam, you hit. Ryan, you're out in the field. We'll switch after every three outs."

The boys took their positions, with Adam standing in the batter's box near the back of the house. A Frisbee was home plate.

Jake's first pitch broke low and away. Adam didn't swing and tossed the ball back.

"Come on, Jake!" Ryan called from the outfield. "No batter, no batter!"

Jake fixed his fingers along the holes in the white plastic ball to throw a big, sweeping curveball. He went into his windup and threw hard. The ball curved sharply toward the strike zone.

Adam whipped the metal bat around in a blur. *Whack!* The ball rocketed forward. Jake ducked to get out of the way, slipped backwards, and ended up sprawled on the grass.

"Are you okay?" Adam asked, moving toward Jake.

"Yeah," Jake said, still lying on his back. "I'm fine."

"I think that's a double," Adam said. He returned to the batter's box.

Ryan jogged in with the ball, barely able to keep himself from laughing. He stood above Jake and dropped the ball on his chest. "I told you he could hit," he said with a grin.

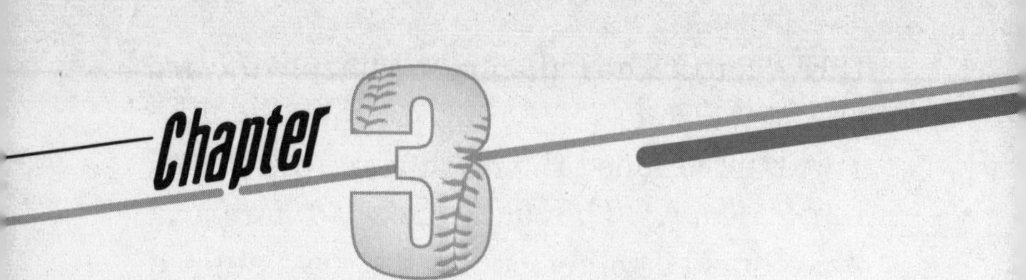

Chapter 3

"Okay, guys, look sharp!" Coach Sanders shouted to his players. He stood at home plate with a bat on his right shoulder and a baseball in his left hand. "Remember, move your feet to get in front of the grounder. Keep your glove low and make a good, solid throw to first base."

Standing in a short line of players at shortstop, Jake nodded. He was ready for infield practice and the chance to show Coach Sanders he could be the Red Sox starting shortstop.

Behind the chain-link backstop, Jake's dad and another assistant coach were throwing soft toss to other players. In the outfield, Ryan's dad was helping out by lofting high fly balls to a third group of Red Sox players.

Coach Sanders isn't fooling around this season, Jake thought as he eyed all the activity on the field. *He's running a pretty serious practice.*

Coach Sanders tossed the ball up and hit a hard, high hopper. Isaiah Slater, who was first in line, stepped in, fielded the ball, and tossed it to Khalil at first base.

"All right. Next player. Be ready," Coach Sanders said as he grabbed another ball from the catcher, Evan, standing beside him. Adam stepped to the front of the line. Coach Sanders smacked a hard grounder that skimmed the infield grass. Adam took a few quick steps to his left, scooped up the grounder, and fired the ball to first base. "Nice play. That's how to move those feet," the coach said. "Jake, you're next."

Jake slid over in front of the bouncing ball. But at the last moment the ball took a high hop. It hit the heel of Jake's glove and fell at his feet. Jake quickly grabbed the ball with his bare hand and threw it to first base.

"Good play. Way to stay with it," Coach Sanders said. "But you've got to field 'em cleaner than that at shortstop," he added.

Jake nodded and moved to the back of the line. He was already one play behind Adam.

As infield practice continued, Jake made most of the plays at shortstop. But Adam made *all* the plays. Grounders to his left, grounders to his right, line drives, pop-ups, it didn't matter. Adam fielded everything like a pro, cool and clean.

And with every one of Adam's great plays, Jake could feel his chances of being the team's starting shortstop fading away. Sure enough, when it came time for Coach Sanders to put together a starting infield, he said, "Okay, why don't we try Isaiah at third, Jake at second, Khalil at first base, and Adam at shortstop?"

Jake felt like he'd been hit by a pitch. *Adam at shortstop!* he thought. *That was supposed to be* my *position!*

He trudged back to second base. Adam might be a big help to the team, but Jake was beginning to think that his new friend could be a big problem for him.

Ryan jogged in from the outfield, heading for the soft-toss station. "What are you doing at second base?" he asked Jake.

"I don't know!" Jake snapped. "Coach put Adam at shortstop."

"Well, he didn't miss a thing in practice," Ryan said.

"I didn't miss many," Jake pointed out.

Ryan shrugged and kept moving.

Adam didn't miss anything during the rest of infield practice, either. And Jake noticed every great play Adam made. He couldn't wait for the end of infield practice.

Jake's group finally moved to soft toss, where Mr. Daley and Isaiah's dad, Mr. Slater, were ready for them. Mr. Daley gave out the batting instructions. "Get your hands back," he said, demonstrating with a strong, smooth swing of the bat. "Make a quick step into the pitch and drive the ball into the net." Then he paused. "Okay, let's see. Jake, you'll start with me; Adam, you can start with Mr. Slater."

Jake stood at the plate, a few feet in front of the net. He almost missed the first toss as it floated in from the side. The bat just nicked the lower edge of the ball and the ball popped weakly over the net.

"Head down. Eyes on the ball, Jake," Mr. Daley said.

Jake got his focus back and began to smack solid line drives into the net—most of the time.

Out of the corner of his eye he could see Adam blasting balls at the other soft-toss station, one right after the other. More important, he could *hear* every one of Adam's hits as his bat connected with the ball and sent it flying dead center into the net. Each hit sounded with the same solid *whack!* as the one before.

A little later, Coach Sanders stood in front of the whole team wearing his usual Boston Red Sox cap, blue with a red *B*. Jake's dad and Isaiah's dad stood behind him. The players took a break on the grass at the edge of the infield, sipping from their water bottles. "I like what I'm seeing out there," Coach Sanders said as he paced the baseline. "We're off to a good start. Everybody's working hard and hustling. The games start in two weeks, on Saturday, April 18. Mr. Daley, will you please hand out the schedules?"

Jake's dad stepped forward and handed a blue sheet of paper to each player.

"When do we get our uniforms?" Kyle asked.

"Next practice, I hope."

Jake glanced at the list of games on the schedule.

Coach Sanders kept talking and pacing. "When the season begins, we'll be playing to win. I'll play people in the positions where I think they can most help the team." The coach paused and looked around at his players. "But I don't want to wear out the pitchers' arms, so no one will pitch more than two or three innings a game. Any questions?"

Jake glanced to his right and then to his left. None of the kids spoke or raised a hand.

RED SOX SCHEDULE

Date	Opponent	Time
Sat. April 18	Braves	2 pm
Wed. April 22	Royals	6:30 pm
Sat. April 25	Yankees	noon
Tues. April 28	Dodgers	6:30 pm
Sat. May 2	Reds	4 pm
Thurs. May 7	Giants	6:30 pm
Sat. May 9	Tigers	10 am
Tues. May 12	Braves	6:30 pm
Sat. May 16	Royals	noon
Sat. May 23	Yankees	2 pm
Wed. May 27	Dodgers	6:30 pm
Sat. May 30	Reds	4 pm
Wed. June 3	Giants	6:30 pm
Sat. June 6	Tigers	noon
Sat. June 13	Championship Game	

"Seems like the Red Sox want to play more than talk," Adam whispered to Jake with a grin. "I like that."

"All right," Coach Sanders said with a clap of his hands. "Let's have some real batting practice now. I'll pitch. Everybody gets ten swings." He started pointing around the field, telling kids where to go. "Adam, you're up first. Jake, you're on deck. Michael's on double deck. Everybody else is out in the field. Let's hustle."

The Red Sox raced to their positions. Adam and Jake picked out bats from the half-dozen lying in the dirt behind the backstop.

"Batter up!" Coach Sanders called from the mound.

Adam stepped up to the plate. He dug his right foot into the dirt and stared out at Coach Sanders. Jake leaned forward against the chain-link backstop and watched Adam's smooth swing send line drives flying into the field, pitch after pitch. Each hit sounded with the same firm *whack!* that Jake had heard when Adam was hitting soft tosses into a net. Then Adam really connected, and the ball rocketed high and deep as the outfielders watched in awe.

"Wow," Michael whispered on the sidelines as the ball soared higher and higher.

But Jake wasn't watching the ball. From

behind the backstop he kept his gaze on Adam. The new player's face was shining in the late afternoon sunlight as he watched the ball fly high and long.

As he eyed Adam, Jake started to worry. *Maybe this isn't going to be my year after all,* he thought.

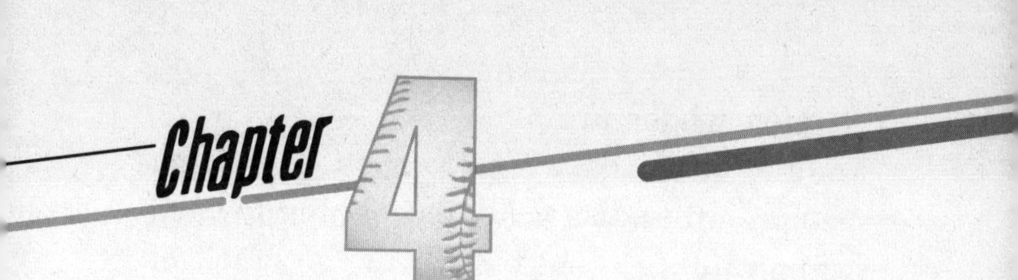

The yellow tennis ball bounced low and hard against the house and then skipped along the well-mowed grass. Jake raced to his right and fielded the bouncing ball backhanded. "Daley makes a great play for the Red Sox, going deep into the hole," he said in his best announcer's voice as he pivoted and fired the ball against the house again.

Thunk! This time the ball bounced high to Jake's left. He scrambled quickly to his glove side and snagged the ball out of the air. "Another great play by Daley!" he shouted in his announcer's voice. "He's the star of the team." Then he flipped another throw at the house.

"Hey, what's up?"

Jake took his eyes from the spinning tennis ball and saw Adam heading toward him, cradling a basketball in the crook of his arm. The tennis ball bounced over Jake's glove. Adam cupped his free hand around his mouth and announced in a loud voice, "Error on the second baseman, Daley."

Jake's lips tightened as he picked up the ball at the back fence. It seemed like Adam was coming over every afternoon now, whether he was invited or not. "You distracted me," Jake protested.

Adam shrugged and held up the basketball. "You want to shoot some hoops?" he asked.

Jake shook his head. "Nah, I gotta practice," he said.

"Why? We don't have practice today. Come on."

Jake threw the ball against the house, but kept talking as he fielded grounders and kept his eyes on the ball.

"Coach Sanders said I've got to field the

ball cleanly if I want to play shortstop," he said. "So I'm practicing grounders."

"I'm gonna be the shortstop," Adam said. "Coach puts me there every infield practice."

"No kidding. But you'll probably pitch a few innings every game. We'll need a shortstop whenever you're pitching," Jake said as he fired another throw against the house. *I'm going to practice so hard, I'll be even better than you!* he added to himself.

The ball bounced back. Jake got in front of it, but he lifted his glove too early and the ball skipped between his legs.

Adam cupped his hand around his mouth again. "Error on the shortstop, Daley," he said, grinning.

Jake didn't think that was funny. He hoped Adam would leave soon.

Just then, Jake's father stepped out the back door. "Oh, hi, Adam. How's your mom?"

"Fine. She's working late." Adam bounced the basketball on the Daleys' patio.

"Do you want to have dinner with us?" Mr. Daley asked.

"What?" Jake said, but his father shot

him a quick watch-your-manners! glance. "We're going to meet Jake's mom at Mi Rancho, a Mexican restaurant downtown."

"Sure," Adam answered without hesitation. "I'll just text my mom."

"We'll be leaving in twenty minutes," Mr. Daley said as he went into the house.

Adam put the basketball down. He texted his mom, pocketed the phone, then held out his right hand. "Come on, I'll throw you some grounders."

"Fine," Jake said. Reluctantly he tossed Adam the tennis ball.

"Okay, you ready?" Adam said. He turned and fired the ball against the house. *Thunk!* The ball skipped along the grass. Jake dashed to his right, reached his glove across his body, and snagged the ball. Then he leaped, twisted in the air, and flipped a hard throw right to Adam. "Nice play." Adam nodded. "Maybe you *will* make it as our starting shortstop."

Fat chance of that with you around, Jake thought.

Less than an hour later, Jake's family

and Adam were sitting around a table covered with a plastic red tablecloth at the small, crowded restaurant. Mr. and Mrs. Daley sat together near one end of the table. Jake, his nine-year-old sister Ivy, and Adam sat at the other. Soon the table filled with easy conversation.

"So, are you boys ready for the first game?" Mr. Daley asked as he helped himself to some beans and rice.

"Yeah," Jake and Adam answered together.

"When is the game?" Mrs. Daley asked.

"Saturday at two o'clock," Jake said. "Please pass the chips."

"Will your mom or dad be at the game, Adam?" Mrs. Daley asked as she handed Jake the chips.

"I don't know," Adam said, looking down at his plate. "I don't think so."

"Do you see your dad much?" Mr. Daley asked. Jake saw his mom give his dad a warning look.

"Not too much," Adam said. "Me and my brother sleep at his apartment sometimes."

Mr. Daley nodded and then changed the

subject. "Think Coach Sanders is going to pitch you on Saturday?"

"I hope so," Adam said, looking up and smiling. "I'll only get to pitch a couple of innings, though. But that's okay, because I like to play in the infield too."

"Are you the best player on the team?" Ivy asked, looking across the table at Adam. Jake glared at his sister.

Mr. Daley spoke before Adam had a chance to answer. "Adam is very good," he said. "But we have a lot of good players on the team. Your brother's been doing a good job at second base. "

"I wish Coach would put me at shortstop, Dad," Jake said.

"We'll see," Mr. Daley said. "Do you boys want some more salsa?"

"Sure," Adam said, reaching for the small bowl.

"Who are you playing on Saturday?" Mrs. Daley asked.

"The Braves," Jake said. "They have Tony DiMichael. He's supposed to be a real good pitcher."

Mr. Daley smiled. "It's too bad Coach Sanders can't pitch for the Braves. Adam's been crushing all his pitches in practice. Last Tuesday, he hit the longest home run I've ever seen."

Jake felt his shoulders tighten.

"Really?" Mrs. Daley smiled. Adam didn't answer. He was busy wolfing down a beef burrito.

"Are you guys going to be better than last year?" Ivy asked.

Adam shrugged as he finished chewing his mouthful of burrito.

"I guess we'll start finding out on Saturday," Jake said.

But with a star like Adam, how could they lose?

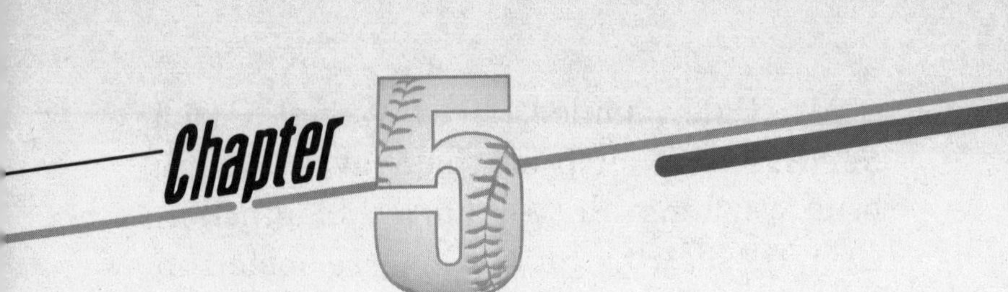

"Okay, Red Sox. Listen up!" Coach Sanders shouted. The team crowded around him. It was Opening Day and the Red Sox were ready to play ball. "It's our first game of the year," the coach went on. "Don't worry, everybody will get a chance to play. Here's the starting lineup. Chris will lead off and play center field. Jake bats second and plays shortstop..."

Shortstop! All right! Jake sat up a bit taller on the bench.

"Adam is pitching and batting third..."

Of course he is, Jake thought. *And Coach will probably put him at shortstop as soon as he's through pitching.*

"...Isaiah's at third base and batting cleanup. Evan, you're catching and batting fifth. Hannah..." Coach Sanders gave out the rest of the lineup and then turned to Mr. Daley. "Did you bring your laptop?" he asked.

"I've got it right here," Jake's dad said, patting the computer bag on his shoulder. "I'll score the game."

"Hey, with your dad keeping the score, he'll probably give you a hit every time," Ryan teased. Jake smiled. He knew his dad wouldn't do that, but he was happy his dad would be around.

The Braves were up first. Adam struck out the first batter with a blazing fastball. The second batter popped up to first base. "Two outs," Jake called to the outfield, holding two fingers over his head. He felt great standing at shortstop.

The next batter hit a high hopper to Jake's right. Jake snagged the ball and threw to first base, but the runner beat the throw. Standing on the mound, Adam turned to Jake. "Don't worry, I've got the next batter," he said. Sure enough, he struck out the Braves clean-up hitter with a sizzling third strike.

"Chris, Jake, Adam, Isaiah…" Mr. Daley called the lineup as the Red Sox came off the field and got ready to hit.

Chris popped out on the first pitch. After a couple of quick practice swings, Jake stepped into the batter's box. Tony DiMichael, the Braves pitcher, threw the first pitch by Jake's late swing.

"Strike one!" the umpire shouted.

Jake stepped out of the batter's box and blew out a deep breath. *I don't want to be the first strikeout of the year,* he thought as he stepped back into the box and looked out at the Braves pitcher. The second pitch was on the outside corner of the plate. Jake swung hard.

Crack! The ball sailed over the second baseman's head for a clean single. The Red Sox bench was up and cheering.

"All right, Daley!"

"There goes your no-hitter, DiMichael."

"Way to be a hitter."

Jake looked back and saw his father entering the hit into his laptop with a smile. His mother and sister were whistling and clapping.

"Come on, Adam, drive me in," Jake shouted to his friend from first base.

At the plate, Adam let the first pitch sail wide. Jake danced off first base and then looked back to the bench. "Be ready to run on a passed ball!" Coach Sanders shouted.

Jake crouched at first base with his left foot on the edge of the bag and his right knee bent. Tony DiMichael reared back and tried to get something extra on the next pitch. Adam unleashed a smooth swing and the ball exploded off the bat.

Jake ran toward second base, but then slowed to a jog as he watched the flight of the ball. The Braves leftfielder took a few steps toward the fence and looked up too. The ball soared twenty feet over the fence. It was a home run! No doubt about it.

Jake rounded the bases inside a circle of cheers. The whole Red Sox team was at home plate. They slapped him on the back and then pushed him away to make room for Adam. The Red Sox home-run slugger was smiling as he jogged around third base. The team mobbed him at home plate with loud cheers and huge hugs.

Adam grabbed Jake by the arm. "Nice hit," he said. "You keep getting on and I'll keep driving you in. We'll make a great team."

Coach Sanders clapped his hands and shouted at the bench. "All right, good job, Adam and Jake. Let's get some more hits. We need more runs."

"Isaiah, you're up," Jake's dad called from the corner of the dugout. "Evan's on deck. Hannah's in the hole."

"We don't need any of you guys," Ryan joked to the upcoming batters. "We've got Adam!"

"We're gonna need everybody," Hannah said as she put on a batting helmet. "Even you, Ryan."

"Are you kidding? I'm going to go get some ice cream," Ryan said. "Adam can win this one all by himself."

"I don't think so," said Jake, shooting a sideways glance at Ryan.

The Red Sox scored another run as Hannah smacked a single that brought Isaiah home. The Red Sox led, 3–0.

Adam pitched another shutout inning in the bottom of the second. The Red Sox didn't score. Coach Sanders brought Sam in to pitch and, sure enough, moved Adam to shortstop and Jake to second base.

Why does Adam have to be so good at everything? Jake thought as he shifted to second. *It isn't fair.* But he had to admit that Adam was really helping the team.

The Braves had an easier time with Sam pitching, scoring two runs in the third inning and adding two more in the fourth. When the Red Sox came to bat in the bottom of the fifth, the Braves led the Red Sox 4–3.

"Come on, we're only down by one," Coach Sanders called as the Red Sox ran off the field and got ready to bat. "We have two more chances to come back. Let's get some runs. Who's up?"

Mr. Daley checked his laptop. "Michael, Kyle, and then the top of the order: Chris, Jake and Adam. Everybody hits."

Michael didn't get a hit, but he did get on base with a walk. Kyle smacked a sharp grounder right at the Braves shortstop, who quickly tagged second base before Michael could get there. One out!

With his foot still on the base, the shortstop fired the ball to first.

"Oh no!" Jake yelled from the bench. It looked like the Braves were going to turn the grounder into a double play. But Kyle hustled down the baseline and beat the throw to first by the blink of an eye. Safe! Runner on first, one out.

"Come on, Chris. Be a hitter!" Jake cheered his teammate as he took a practice swing in the on-deck circle.

The Red Sox center fielder came through with a bloop single to left field. So Jake stepped into the batter's box with Kyle on second and Chris on first base. One out. The pressure was on and Jake felt the excitement building. *This is my big chance to be a hero,* Jake told himself as he watched the Braves pitcher go into his windup.

The first pitch was a little high. Jake swung and lifted the ball high above the Braves infield. He took a few steps toward first base, but saw the Braves second baseman settling under the pop-up. The ball fell easily into the second baseman's glove. Jake slammed his bat into the dirt and trudged off the field. He dropped onto the Red Sox bench and buried his head in his hands.

"Don't worry," Ryan said cheerfully. "We've still got Adam up. He'll get a hit."

"Will you stop talking about Adam all the time?" Jake snapped at his friend. "What if he *doesn't* come through?"

Ryan looked at Jake as if Jake were crazy. "What are the chances of that?" he said.

Crack! Adam drilled a line drive deep into center field.

"Whoa, did you see that, Jake?" Ryan shouted as he jumped off the bench. The Braves raced frantically toward the ball.

When Jake saw Kyle race across home

plate with the tying run, he jumped up too. Everyone was cheering as Chris rounded third base right behind Kyle. The Braves shortstop pegged a relay throw to home plate, hoping to get him. But the ball skipped by the catcher and Chris slid in with the go-ahead run.

Adam had come through again. The Red Sox led, 5–4.

"Told you!" Ryan shouted above the cheers. "Adam *always* comes through."

The Red Sox added another hit and another run. They raced out onto the field in the last inning with a two-run lead.

The Braves made two quick outs. Then Jake dashed toward the first-base foul line and snagged a pop fly for the last out. He turned toward the infield and happily held up the ball, still tight in his glove. At shortstop, Adam pointed at Jake and shouted, "Great catch!"

The Red Sox had won their first game of the season, 6–4.

Later, Jake and his father sat on a bench away from the field, checking the game stats on Mr. Daley's laptop. "You got one hit in four times at bat," Mr. Daley said. "You scored a run and made a nice play to end the game."

Jake nodded. "How did Adam do?" he asked.

"Well, let's see. He got three hits in four at bats. He scored two runs and had four runs batted in. And he pitched two scoreless innings." Mr. Daley smiled as he closed his laptop. "Not bad."

Yeah, Jake thought. *Just bad for me.*

Chapter 6

"Okay, let's get two!" Coach Sanders shouted, trying to get his infield focused on making double plays. Then he slapped a hard ground ball to Jake at second base. Jake slid over as Adam rushed to cover second. Jake scooped up the ball and flipped it underhanded to Adam.

Adam caught it easily, tagged second base with his foot, and fired the ball to first.

"Great play!" Coach Sanders said. "*Now* we're looking like a team that's seven and one."

Standing back at second, Jake thought about the Red Sox season so far. Seven wins and only one loss. They were off to a great start. But he was still hoping to get more chances to play shortstop. He wanted to be the starting shortstop even when Adam wasn't pitching. He'd worked on his fielding at home almost every day for weeks. Now, at practice, Jake figured he would take a chance. He called over in a loud whisper to Adam, "Hey, Adam, would it be okay if I asked Coach to switch us? You play second and I play shortstop?"

"Go for it," Adam replied with a shrug.

"Hey, Coach," Jake called during a pause in infield practice. "Can Adam and me switch positions for a few turns?"

Coach Sanders looked out at the infield. "Okay, let's try it."

Jake and Adam did a quick fist bump as they switched positions. Coach Sanders grabbed another baseball and swung the bat up onto his shoulder. "Let's get two."

This time Adam fielded the ball at second base and flipped it to Jake, running over from shortstop to cover the bag. Jake caught it easily, but his nervous throw to first was low and skipped under the first baseman's glove.

"Again," Coach Sanders called. The new infield combination was all right, but just all right. Jake made a couple of errors and had to admit that things were not as smooth as when Adam was at shortstop and he was at second base.

"Okay, that's enough infield for now," Coach Sanders said, holding up the bat. He walked over to Jake and Adam as the boys jogged off the field. "I think we'd better leave it the way it was," he said. "You know, Adam at shortstop and Jake at second. You guys are a pretty good team that way."

Tight-lipped, Jake nodded. All his practice at home had not paid off. Adam was still the best shortstop. Coach Sanders put a hand on Jake's shoulder. "You can play shortstop when Adam is pitching," he said. Then he turned back to the rest of the team. "Okay, everybody switch. Mr. Daley's group over here and my group over there."

Jake's dad gave the usual batting instructions as the boys stepped up to the soft-toss station. "Hands back. Quick step. Keep your eyes on the ball."

Adam was up first. He thundered line drive after line drive into the practice net.

"The ball even sounds different coming off his bat," Jake whispered to his dad as Mr. Daley lofted Adam another soft-toss pitch from the side of the plate.

"Don't worry about Adam," Mr. Daley said. "Concentrate on your own swing."

Adam swung hard and cracked another line drive into the net. "Good," Mr. Daley said.

"Hey, Adam!" a voice called. Adam's mom stood at the edge of the practice area. She was tall with dark hair, just like Adam. "I'm going to pick up your brother in a half hour."

Adam stood back with the bat on his shoulder. "Okay," he said, and then drilled the next pitch into the net.

Mrs. Hull looked at Jake's dad. "Do you think Adam could go home with you guys?"

"Sure, no problem," Mr. Daley said. "Do you want us to give him dinner?"

Mrs. Hull shook her head. "No, thanks, that's all right. I'll pick him up by six." She waved good-bye and walked toward the parking lot at the edge of the field beyond the outfield.

"Okay, that's enough soft toss for you guys," Mr. Daley said with a wave. "Let's move on to batting practice. Coach Sanders is pitching."

A car skidded to a loud stop in the parking lot. A man opened the door and stepped out.

"Uh-oh," Adam said softly.

"Who's that guy?" Jake asked.

"My dad." Adam sounded tired.

"I thought you said he didn't come around much," Jake said.

"He doesn't," Adam said. "But when he does, it's usually trouble. My mom and dad don't get along too good."

Jake leaned on his bat and watched Adam's father walk up to Adam's mother. The two stood a few feet apart. Mr. Hull started pacing back and forth, frowning and waving his hands. Mrs. Hull stood still with her arms crossed. Jake could tell they were arguing, but they were too far away for him to hear what they were saying.

Mr. Daley got up from where he was throwing soft toss. "You guys go hit," he said to Jake and Adam. "I'll be back in a minute." Then he walked down the left-field foul line and up to the Hulls. The three adults spoke and Adam's parents moved farther away from the field. Mr. Daley walked back to the batting practice area.

Jake stood at the on-deck circle. Adam was watching his parents as they headed toward the parking lot, still arguing and pointing at each other.

Jake caught Adam's eye. His friend managed a small smile and shrugged. The two boys didn't say a word.

"Come on, Adam, you're up. Let's go," Coach Sanders called from the pitcher's mound. Adam put on a batter's helmet and stepped into the batter's box.

Mr. Daley stood next to Jake in the on-deck circle. "What's going on, Dad?" Jake asked.

"Oh, I don't know. They're just discussing a few things," Mr. Daley said. "Let's focus on practice."

Jake turned and watched Adam at the plate. The Red Sox star player was swinging too hard, as if he wanted to crush every pitch. He popped up the first four pitches.

"Just meet it," Coach Sanders said between pitches. "You've got plenty of power. Don't try to kill it."

Adam stepped out of the box, moved his hands around the bat handle, and took a deep breath. Jake glanced out at the parking lot. The Hulls were still arguing, even more heatedly than before. On the next pitch, Adam swung slower and smoother, more like the old Adam. The ball flew off the bat, far over the left fielder's head. The ball took a high, hard bounce and skimmed across the parking lot, just a few feet away from Adam's parents.

But the Hulls didn't notice the ball. They didn't even turn when the outfielder scrambled by. They just kept arguing.

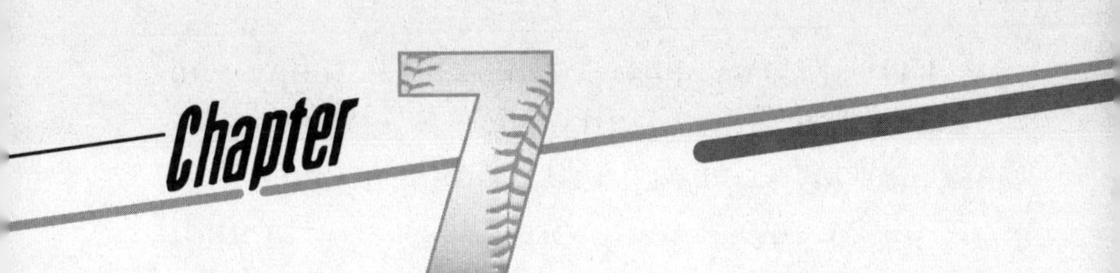

"Chris, Jake, Adam, Isaiah..." Coach Sanders called out the familiar lineup as the Red Sox listened on the bench. "Kyle's sick today, so Ryan will start in right field and bat ninth."

"All right!" Jake smiled at his friend. "You're in the starting lineup."

"Yeah," the Red Sox benchwarmer said. "But I'm way out in right field."

"So what?" Jake said. "Babe Ruth played right field."

"So that means I'm Babe Ruth?" Ryan joked.

"Maybe," Jake replied. Then he jumped up from the bench, clapping his hands.

"Come on, we gotta really hustle today," he said. "The Royals are good."

"What's their record?" Adam asked.

"Five wins and three losses," Hannah answered from the end of the bench. "They just lost to the Dodgers by one run last week."

"Yeah," Jake said. "And the Dodgers are tied with us for first place."

"Who cares?" Ryan said. "We've got Adam on our side, remember?"

"*Everybody's* got to play well," Jake insisted.

"Even Ryan?" Adam gave Ryan a quick shoulder punch.

"Especially Ryan," Jake said. "He's starting today."

The Royals were just as good as Jake thought. They set down the Red Sox in the top of the first inning with three smart fielding plays. In the bottom of the inning, Adam struck out the first two batters. Then the Royals rallied, rapping out two hard hits. They now had runners on second and third, with two outs.

"Come on, Red Sox!" Jake yelled as he pounded his glove out at shortstop. "Let's get the last out."

The Royals runners were off as the batter lifted a high fly ball to right field. Jake watched helplessly as Ryan circled, wobbly legged, under the ball. At the last instant, he stuck out his glove. The ball plopped into the webbing.

"All right!" Jake shouted, throwing his fist into the air.

He turned and caught Adam's eye on the mound. The Red Sox pitcher grinned and let out a big sigh of relief. The score was still 0–0.

The Red Sox tumbled back onto the bench. "Great catch, Ryan," Adam said. "You had me worried for a second."

Ryan dismissed Adam with a wave of his glove. "No problem," he said. "Just call me Babe Ruth."

Jake smiled and rolled his eyes.

The Red Sox and the Royals stayed locked in a tight, tough game. The Red Sox grabbed the lead in the top of the third inning as Jake got on base with a sharp single and Adam sent him racing home with a hard double.

Adam had pitched two innings, so Coach Sanders brought in Sam to pitch. Again he moved Adam to shortstop and Jake to second base. The Royals took advantage of the new pitcher and picked up two runs with a walk and a couple of clean hits. They would have scored even more, but Adam jumped high to snag a scorching line drive for the last out of the inning.

Both teams scored runs in the fourth inning, so the Red Sox trailed 3–2 when they came to bat in the top of the fifth. Ryan and Chris struck out to start the inning. Jake stepped into the batter's box with nobody on and two outs.

"Come on, Jake," Adam cheered from the on-deck circle. "Save my ups."

Jake eyed the infield. The Royals third baseman was playing way back, almost on the edge of the outfield grass. *Two outs, nobody on,* Jake thought. *It might be worth a try...*

The Royals pitcher fired a fastball toward the inside half of the plate. Jake lowered his bat and the ball plunked against it. He sprinted to first base as the ball dribbled slowly toward the third baseman and settled on the infield grass. It was a perfect bunt! Jake was on first and Adam was coming to bat.

Adam won't bunt, Jake told himself as he stood on first base. Sure enough, after two pitches sailed wide, Adam got a pitch that he liked.

Crack! The ball soared over the centerfield wall as Jake and Adam jogged around the bases to put the Red Sox back in the lead, 4–3. The team mobbed Adam at home plate, slapping him on his batting helmet and back.

"Did you see that homer?" Ryan crowed.

"It must have gone a mile," Isaiah said.

"Come on, guys, the game's not over," Jake reminded his teammates. He was annoyed that everyone had forgotten his bunt single. "The Royals aren't going to give up."

The Royals didn't quit. In the bottom of the fifth with Isaiah pitching now, the Royals scratched out another run. The score was tied at 4–4 when the Red Sox came to bat in the sixth and final inning.

"Come on, we're in a real ballgame here," Coach Sanders said as he marched back and forth in front of the bench. "Let's get some more runs."

He stopped in front of Adam and Jake. "How's your arm feeling?" he asked Adam.

"Fine."

Coach Sanders turned to Jake's father, who was sitting in the corner of the dugout. "How many pitches did Adam throw in the first two innings?" he asked.

Mr. Daley studied his laptop screen for a moment. "Thirty-four," he answered. "He's nowhere near the seventy-five-pitch limit."

Coach Sanders turned back to Adam. "I may need you to come back and pitch the sixth inning if we get ahead. Can you do it?"

"No problem," Adam said.

All the Red Sox were up and cheering when Michael smacked a solid single to center field. Hannah dashed toward home with the go-ahead run.

The Red Sox were back on top, 5–4. "Listen up," Coach Sanders called as the Red Sox got ready to take the field. "Adam's going back in to pitch. Jake's going to short-stop. Michael to second base. Great hit, Michael. Now let's hold them."

Jake stood at shortstop and watched Adam warm up. His easy, almost effortless delivery sent the ball speeding to Evan's mitt.

Sssssssmack!

The Royals don't stand a chance now, Jake said to himself, shaking his head and smiling.

Adam blew fastballs by the first two batters, striking out each of them on three straight pitches. The final Royals hitter looped a lazy pop fly to shortstop. Jake caught it easily and held the ball high above his head in triumph.

The Red Sox had won, 5–4! The bench filled with high fives and happy chatter.

After they collected their gloves and

equipment bags, Jake, Adam, and Ryan walked together toward the parking lot.

"That was close," Jake said. "The Royals were tough."

"I knew we'd win," Adam said.

"How'd you know that?" Jake asked.

Adam jerked a thumb at Ryan. "When Ryan caught that fly ball in the first inning, I figured it was our lucky day."

"Just call me Babe Ruth," Ryan said.

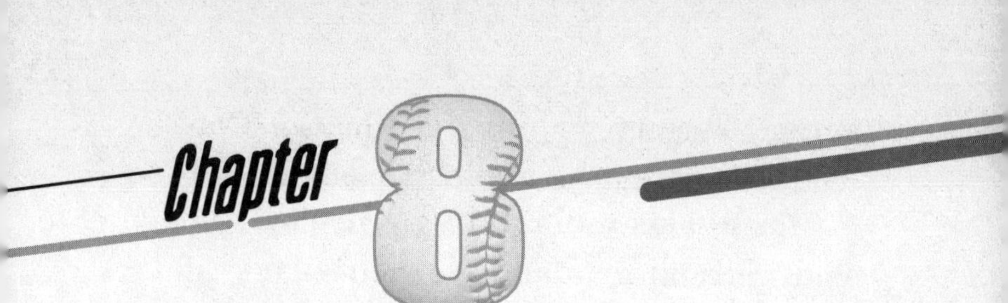

Chapter 8

Jake stared at the back of his house. He took two steps forward and threw the tennis ball hard against it.

Thwack! The ball flew high in the air. Keeping his eye on the ball, Jake drifted back until he was almost at the back fence. The ball was headed into the next yard, but he ripped it from the air with a quick snap of his glove.

"Nice catch. Are you trying to be our center fielder now?"

Adam stood at the corner of the yard, a backpack slung over his shoulder.

"Hey, what's up?" Jake said.

"I forgot my key," Adam said with a

shrug. "I can't get into my house. Can I hang out here for a while?"

"You're always forgetting your key!" Jake said. "I'll tell my dad." He went inside and made his way downstairs to his father's office. "Adam's here," he announced. "He forgot his keys. Again."

Mr. Daley raised one eyebrow. "You don't sound too thrilled," he said.

"I don't care. It's just that he's always coming over," Jake said. "First he takes over the team and then he takes over my house."

Mr. Daley pushed back his desk chair and stood up. "Give Adam a break," he said. "He's new in town and new on the team. That's not easy."

"I guess," Jake said.

"Come on," Mr. Daley said, putting his arm around Jake. "Let's go upstairs."

Jake and his dad went out into the yard. "Hi, Adam," Mr. Daley said. "It's nice to see you."

"I forgot my key," Adam explained. "I just texted my mom. She's going to leave work early and pick me up here, if that's okay."

"That's no problem," Mr. Daley said. Then he turned to his son. "Right, Jake?" he asked. But it really wasn't a question.

"Um, sure," Jake said.

Jake watched his dad go back into the house. Then he looked at Adam. "So what do you want to do?"

"What were you doing?" Adam said.

"Practicing," Jake answered. He tossed the tennis ball in the air and caught it. "Hey, let's play Outs. We haven't played that before."

"What's Outs?"

Jake began to explain the game as he walked around the backyard pointing. "Okay, one guy is in the field and the guy with the ball is the batter."

"Where's the bat?" Adam asked, looking around.

"No bat. The batter just throws the ball against the house, like when I practice grounders," Jake said. He pretended to throw the ball at the house. "The fielder has to stand back here," he went on, turning and walking farther into the yard. "Any grounder that gets by the fielder is a single. Anything that lands in the yard past the bush is a double."

"What's a triple?" Adam asked.

"If it hits the fence on the fly," Jake answered, pointing. "Anything over the fence is a home run."

"That's real far," Adam said, looking at the fence. "How can you get a home run?"

"Oh, there are ways." Jake smiled as he thought of a certain uneven spot on the house. "But I'm not telling you. That's my home-field advantage."

"Come on," Adam said. "You've already got a big advantage. I don't even have my glove."

"We can share my glove. We only need one." Jake flipped Adam the tennis ball. "You're up first," he said.

The game was low scoring. Both boys were fast and good fielders. Not many "hits" got by them or fell onto the grass. Jake scored first when Adam bobbled a hot grounder.

"That's an error," Jake said. "So I'm ahead, 1–0."

"It's your lousy glove," Adam said, smashing

his fist into the leather. "You should put some oil in the pocket. It's too stiff."

"It wasn't so stiff when you made that diving stop last inning," Jake pointed out.

Adam pulled ahead in the top of the last inning when the ball angled away from Jake's outstretched glove for a double. That drove in two runs.

After Jake caught a high fly ball at the fence for the third out, he tossed Adam his glove.

"Okay, it's the bottom of the last inning. You're ahead, 2–1," Jake said. "I've got last ups."

"So now you're gonna bring out your secret home-run ball," Adam said. He slipped his left hand into Jake's glove.

"Home-field advantage," Jake said with a smile. Then he turned to look at the house. *First I'd better get someone on base,* he thought. Jake tried a hard, high throw, but Adam moved quickly to his left, reached up, and snagged the ball.

"One out," Adam said, tossing the ball back to Jake.

Jake ran a few steps toward the house, leaned to his left, and threw hard and low to his right. The fake worked. The grounder skipped just past the diving Adam for a single.

"Nice hit," Adam said. "Are you gonna bring out your secret home-run ball now?"

Jake looked up at the house for his special spot. He knew if he threw the ball too high or too low it wouldn't make it to the fence. But if he hit his spot at the right angle, the ball would fly over the fence and he would finally beat Adam at something.

"One out, one runner on," Jake said, making sure Adam knew he had two chances to come back.

"Oh no." Adam grinned. "I'm in trouble now. How far back can I play?"

"You have to start even with the bush," Jake said, pointing to the side of the yard. He looked back at the house, eyed his spot, then took two steps forward and threw hard. His throw was a little off and the ball floated too high.

Adam raced back and said in his best

announcer voice, "It's a long drive. Hull is going back...back...back. He has room, and he...makes the catch!"

Adam threw the ball to Jake. "Daley's down to his last at bat," he said, still using his announcer's voice. "Hull leads by one run."

Jake fixed his eyes on his special spot again. He took two steps and threw. This time, the ball hit its mark at just the right angle and flew high into the afternoon sky. Jake turned, certain he had his home run and his victory.

Adam sprinted to the fence. This time there was no announcer's voice. He turned and leaped, stretching his gloved hand back over the fence as far as he could. The ball disappeared. Adam bounced off the fence and tumbled to the ground with his glove, now closed, underneath him. He got up slowly and walked in with his hands hanging at his sides, his glove still shut tight.

Jake ran toward Adam with both fists held high in triumph like a boxer who had just scored a knockout. "I win!" he declared. "Finally."

"Not so fast," Adam said. He opened his glove and tossed the yellow tennis ball to Jake. "*I* win," he said with a smile. "Two to one."

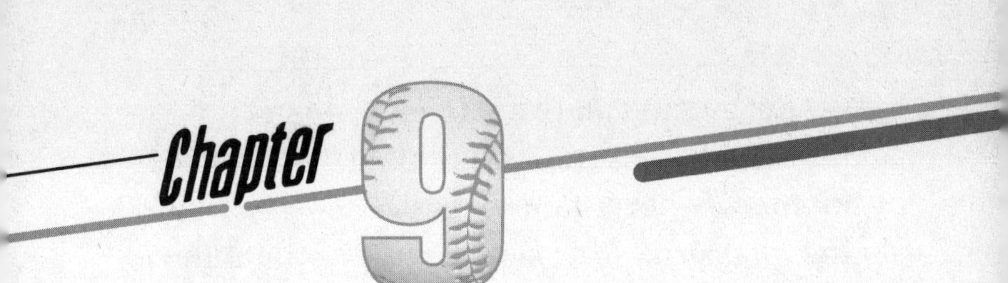

Chapter 9

"Wh...what?" Jake stammered. "There's no way you caught that ball."

"Then how did it get in my glove?" Adam asked, still smiling.

"I can't believe it!" Jake screamed, slapping the sides of his legs. "I can't beat you at *anything.*"

Just then Adam's cell phone rang and he pulled it from his pocket.

"Hi, Mom...yeah...okay. Love ya. Bye." He turned to Jake. "My mom says she'll be here in twenty minutes."

Oh no, Jake thought. *Twenty more minutes playing Outs with Adam.*

"Let's get something to eat," Jake said.

"Sure." Adam followed him inside to the kitchen, where Jake's sister Ivy was making popcorn. Mr. Daley sat at the table, reading something on his laptop.

"Hi, guys. How's it going?" Mr. Daley said.

"Adam's mom is picking him up soon," Jake was quick to point out.

"Okay," Mr. Daley said.

Jake squeezed tight on the tennis ball as he glanced at his father and then at Adam.

"Is everything all right?" Mr. Daley asked, looking at Jake.

"Yeah." Jake nodded. "Everything's fine." *Except I can't wait for Adam to leave,* he added to himself.

"So Adam, how many home runs have you hit this season?" Mr. Daley asked, filling the awkward silence.

"I don't know," Adam said. "A bunch, I guess."

"I have the team stats right here," Mr. Daley said as he pulled them up on his computer. "I think you have at least five."

"I saw one," Ivy blurted out, as she emptied the warm bag of popcorn into a bowl. "You hit it really far."

"Dad, I thought you didn't like us looking at our stats before the end of the season," Jake reminded his father.

"I'm just curious," Mr. Daley said. He studied the numbers on his screen. "Yep, I was right. You have five home runs. You're batting over .600 and you have twenty-four runs batted in." He leaned back and shook his head. "You've had one terrific season already, Adam, and it isn't over."

"Hey, Ivy, can I have some of that popcorn?" Jake asked. He wasn't interested in talking about Adam's stats.

"You're hitting really well, and you're pitching great too," Mr. Daley said. "Which do you like better?"

"I like them both, I guess," Adam said. "I just like to play."

"Well, after high school more than 40 percent of the players are pitchers. So you may want to concentrate on pitching. You might even get a college scholarship."

Bing-bong. The Daleys' doorbell rang, and Mrs. Hull rushed in with Adam's little brother Chad tagging along.

"Is everything all right?" Mr. Daley asked.

"Oh, fine...fine," she answered, a bit out of breath. "I just wanted to get here quickly. I worry about Adam wearing out his welcome."

"He's no problem at all," Mr. Daley said. "The boys have fun together."

Just then Jake's mom walked into the kitchen. "Oh, hi," she said to Mrs. Hull and Chad. "How are you?"

"Good, thanks," Mrs. Hull said. She looked from Mrs. Daley to Mr. Daley and back again. "I was wondering whether Jake might like to sleep over at our house tonight?"

Mr. and Mrs. Daley exchanged glances. "Are you sure that's okay?" Mrs. Daley asked. "You'll have your hands full with three boys."

Mrs. Hull laughed. "I already have my hands full with two. Besides, you've both been so good to Adam, this is a way for me to say thanks."

"Yeah, it'll be cool," Adam said to Jake. "I'll show you my room. We can watch a movie and—"

"We've, um, got a big game tomorrow," Jake said softly.

Mr. Daley glanced up at the schedule posted on the refrigerator behind a thick magnet. "The game isn't until noon," he said. "So you boys should be able to get plenty of sleep." He looked at Mrs. Hull. "Should Jake bring a sleeping bag?"

"No, we have plenty."

"Jake can sleep in my bed if he wants," Adam said. "I can sleep on the floor."

Jake stood in the middle of everyone, feeling as if he were invisible. He didn't want to sleep over at Adam's house. The truth was that Jake was tired of Adam. He was tired of him always hanging around after school, tired of him always being the star of the team, and tired of him being better than Jake at everything. Even Outs.

"So how about it?" Mrs. Hull smiled at

Jake. "Would you like to be one of the Hull brothers for a night?"

No, Jake wanted to say. But he knew he didn't really have a choice.

Mrs. Hull pulled into the driveway and turned off the car lights.

"Come on, Jake, you've never seen my house," Adam said as he bounced out of the car. "I want to show you my room."

Jake got out of the car slowly and looked at the Hulls' house. It was smaller than Jake's. Large, overgrown bushes hid some of the windows and the grass on the front lawn was high.

"Wait just a minute," Mrs. Hull said. "Could you boys help with the grocery bags?" Adam and Jake grabbed the two bags and Chad followed close behind as they all walked up to the front door. "You'll have to excuse the house," Mrs. Hull said to Jake as she turned the key in the lock. "I haven't had time to pick up." She turned on a light and stepped into a messy kitchen. Dishes and glasses were piled in the sink and along the counter. The pale green refrigerator was covered with photos of Adam and Chad.

Adam's mom set her purse down on the crowded counter and started to put the groceries away. She pulled a frozen pizza from one of the bags. "I'll put this in the oven for you guys," she said, as a large black dog bounded into the kitchen. Jake stepped back.

"Oh, that's just Fenway," she said. "Don't worry, he's very friendly. Adam, be sure to get him outside soon. I don't want him to pee on the rug again."

Adam scratched Fenway behind the ears. The dog's large pink tongue slipped out of his mouth and his tail wagged. Jake took a half step forward and let the dog nuzzle his hand, then petted the dog's head. Fenway licked his hand.

"What kind of dog is he?" Jake asked.

"I don't know," Mrs. Hull answered. "We got him from the pound."

"He's a mutt," Adam said. "My dad calls him an all-American dog."

"Why don't you go show Jake your room, Adam?" Mrs. Hull suggested.

The boys walked through a small living room that had a television, a large couch, and two folding chairs. Down the hall, Jake saw two bedrooms next to each other.

"That's my mom's room," Adam said, pointing. "And this is where me and Chad sleep."

He flicked on the overhead light. Twin beds were pressed against opposite walls. A dresser with a pile of clothes on top was at one end of the room. Sports posters were taped to the walls. A rug with the helmets of all thirty-two National Football League teams covered the floor between the beds.

Coming up behind the boys, Mrs. Hull said, "Jake, you can sleep in a sleeping bag on the floor between the beds," she said. "Or maybe Adam or Chad could give you his bed."

"I'll sleep on the floor," Adam offered quickly.

"I wanna sleep on the floor," Chad whined.

Mrs. Hull held up her hands. "Maybe we should let Chad sleep in between you two. So what do you boys want to do tonight?"

"I figured we'd watch *Major League*." Adam turned to Jake. "Ever seen it?"

"No."

"It's cool. Come on."

"The pizza should be done soon. I'll bring it to you as soon as it's ready," Mrs. Hull said.

A few minutes later, all three boys were sitting on the couch, watching the movie and eating pizza. Fenway lay in a ball on the floor and Mrs. Hull cleaned up the kitchen. Jake heard a loud knock on the door and looked up from the movie.

Mrs. Hull stopped working and glanced over at Adam. She pulled back a shade from the small window by the door. Letting out a long breath, she opened the door a crack. "What do you want?" she asked in a flat voice.

"Oh, this is a good part," Chad said, pointing at the TV. But Jake could see that Adam was watching the door, not the movie. Mrs. Hull opened it wider. A tall man wearing a baseball hat and a gray sweatshirt stepped into the kitchen.

"Dad!" Chad shouted. "Is it next weekend?"

"No," Mr. Hull said, smiling. "I just have to talk to your mother, okay?"

"Okay with me," Adam answered with the same flat voice as his mother's.

Mr. and Mrs. Hull sat at the kitchen table, talking. The boys kept watching the movie. Adam stared at the TV, but he wasn't laughing.

Jake heard bits of the Hulls' conversation above the movie.

"...what about me?"

"...who do you think is going to pay for this?"

"I told you, I didn't want..."

Their voices grew louder, the harsh whispers clashing with the happy sounds of the movie.

"Keep your voice down," Mrs. Hull said finally. "Adam has a friend over." She glanced toward the boys. "Your dad and I are going out onto the back steps."

Adam nodded. Mrs. Hull stepped out first. Mr. Hull looked back. "I'll see you guys next weekend."

"See you, Dad," Chad said, waving.

"I'll try to make one of your games this week, Adam," Mr. Hull added.

"Okay," Adam said. "See ya, Dad."

Mr. Hull stayed in the doorway. "How's the team doing, anyway?"

Adam brightened. "If we win tomorrow, we'll be in the championship game."

"Hey, that's great," Mr. Hull said, then stepped outside. The door closed, but Jake could still hear Adam's parents' voices above the movie. Adam grabbed a pillow off the sofa and pulled it tight across his chest.

The voices outside grew louder.

"...what if I say no?"

"I don't care. I've made up my mind."

"Have you talked to them?"

Jake looked over at Adam. His friend

quickly glanced away and pulled the pillow even tighter.

Mrs. Hull stepped back into the kitchen alone and called to the living room: "You boys go to bed right after the movie. Don't stay up late, you have a game tomorrow. And remember to brush your teeth."

Later, Chad lay in his sleeping bag on the rug between the two boys. He kept talking about the movie. Adam didn't say much. "I'm pretty tired," he said finally and turned toward the wall. "Good night."

Jake drifted off to sleep but woke up a few hours later. He could hear the soft rhythms of Adam and Chad breathing in the darkness. The digital clock on the dresser said 1:38. Jake tossed back the covers and tiptoed carefully around Chad. He noticed there was a light still on in the living room.

Mrs. Hull sat on the couch. The television was off and Fenway was sleeping on the floor.

"Who is it?" Mrs. Hull asked as Jake stepped out of the bedroom.

"Just me, Mrs. Hull," Jake said, peeking into the living room.

"Are you okay, honey?"

"I just woke up, that's all," Jake said. "I have to go to the bathroom."

"Do you know where it is?"

"Yeah. Thanks."

Mrs. Hull looked at Jake with tired eyes. "I guess this house isn't like your house," she said.

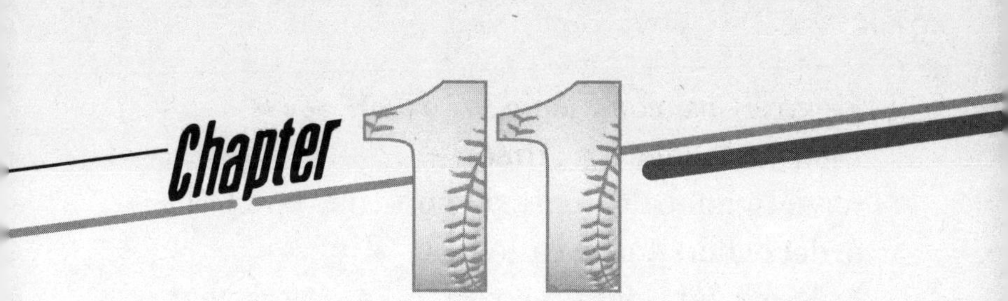

The Red Sox ran toward the bench.

"Come on, everybody, we can come back," Coach Sanders said. "We're only down one run."

Jake glanced at the scoreboard beyond the center-field fence.

INNING	1	2	3	4	5	6
Tigers	0	1	0	1		
Red Sox	1	0	0			

One run down in the bottom of the fourth, he thought as he pounded his fist into his glove. *If we come back and win, we'll be in the championship game.*

"Michael, Kyle, and then the top of the order," Jake's dad called.

Ryan sat down next to Jake. "No sweat, we're gonna win," he said. "We've still got Adam." He looked around. "Hey, where is Adam?"

Jake looked down the bench. His friend was sitting at the very end. He didn't look happy. Jake got up and went over to sit next to him. "Hey, are you okay?" he asked.

Adam shrugged and craned his neck toward the left-field line. Jake looked down the line and saw Mr. Hull leaning against the side of the metal stands. "Hey, your dad's here," Jake said.

"Yeah," Adam said. "Hope my mom doesn't show up."

"Don't worry," Jake said as he pushed off the bench. "Come on, we've got a game to win." He turned around to the field and shouted, "Let's go, Michael, start us off."

Michael smacked a quick comebacker to the pitcher for the first out. But Kyle blooped a pop fly over the shortstop's head for a single. The Red Sox had a runner on first base with one out.

Jake took a few steps and looked back at Adam. He was staring out toward the field but not cheering. Tucked in the corner of the Red Sox bench, Adam didn't seem so big and confident anymore.

Chris struck out swinging, so there were two outs when Jake stepped into the batter's box.

"Remember, Jake, swing level," his dad called from the bench. "Come on, Adam, grab a helmet. You're on deck."

Jake let the first pitch go by. "Strike one," the umpire called. Jake stepped out of the batter's box, took a deep breath, and dug in again.

His father shouted encouragement. "Only takes one. Just like in practice. You can do it, Jake."

Jake met an inside fastball and sent a line drive sizzling down the left-field baseline. Fair ball!

He raced to first base and then sped

toward second. The left fielder went deep into the left-field corner, caught the ball on a bounce, and fired it back into the infield. Kyle slid safe into third base. Now the Red Sox had runners at second and third and two outs, with Adam coming to bat. "Bring us in!" Jake shouted, clapping his hands at second base.

The first pitch cut the heart of the plate. Adam started to swing, but held back. Strike one.

Even out at second base, Jake could hear Adam's father's voice above the noise of the crowd. "Come on, swing the bat. Be ready. Don't be a looker."

Adam tried to kill the next pitch but swung under it, just grazing the bottom of the ball with the top of his bat. The ball flew above the infield, a harmless pop-up to shortstop. Jake jogged without hope to third base.

The shortstop caught the ball for the third out.

"Come on, Adam. What kind of swing was that?" Mr. Hull shouted.

Jake really felt sorry for Adam now. His friend's shoulders were slumped as he headed back to the bench for his glove.

The Red Sox were still behind by a run. The score stayed that way for the next inning and a half. "Last ups and final inning!" Coach Sanders shouted as the Red Sox got ready to bat in the bottom of the sixth. "We need base runners. Who's on deck?"

Mr. Daley called out the batting order. "Khalil. Michael. Kyle. Start us off."

Khalil slapped a hard grounder to the left side of the infield. The Tigers third baseman scooped it up and made a strong throw to first base. One out.

Michael hit another ground ball, but this one found a hole between the first and second basemen. He dashed to first base.

The Red Sox had a runner on! The players bounced off the bench and started cheering like crazy. All the players except Adam. Jake looked back and saw his friend still sitting there. But Jake couldn't worry about Adam right now. The Red Sox were fighting to come back.

Coach Sanders flashed a signal and Kyle laid a perfect bunt down the third-base line. The Tigers third baseman barehanded the ball and threw off-balance to first base. The ball skipped a few yards past the first baseman and the Red Sox runners hustled to move up a base. The Red Sox now had runners at second and third, with one out.

"Chris is up. Jake's on deck. Adam, you're in the hole," Mr. Daley shouted.

The Tigers coach called a time-out and walked out to talk to his pitcher and catcher. After a short conference, the coach headed back to the Tigers bench. The catcher stood and held his glove wide of the plate. Jake frowned. It looked as if the Tigers were walking Chris on purpose to load up the bases.

Sure enough, the pitcher threw four straight balls. Chris ran to first base. The bases were loaded with one out.

Jake was coming to bat with a chance to win the game—and get his team into the championship.

He stood in the on-deck circle between Coach Sanders and his father. "The bases are loaded, Jake," Coach Sanders said. "So there are force plays at every base. Remember, the pitcher has to throw strikes, so look those pitches over."

Jake nodded, wondering if his coach could hear his heart pounding.

His dad patted Jake on the back. "Don't worry," he said in a low voice. "You're a strong hitter. Just get some good swings. Remember, you have Adam in back of you."

Jake took a long, deep breath and stepped into the batter's box. *This is my big chance to help the team,* he thought. *I'm not going to leave it to Adam.*

The Tigers pitcher fired fastballs on the first two pitches. Jake just missed and fouled both pitches back onto the screen behind home plate.

No balls, two strikes.

"Good swing, Jake!" his dad shouted. "You're a hitter. It only takes one."

The pitcher threw another fastball. Jake was a little late but still got the barrel of the bat on the ball. *Crack!*

The ball sliced over the second baseman's

head into right field. The base runners were off as the field filled with cheers.

Jake saw the ball drop onto the outfield grass and spin to the foul line, away from the right fielder. *All right!* Jake thought, his heart and feet racing. *My hit may drive in two runs!* He turned the corner at first base and looked toward home. The Tigers catcher stood helplessly near the plate with his mask off as Michael dashed across home plate. Kyle motored in right behind him with the winning run.

The Red Sox had won. They were in the championship game! The team mobbed Kyle at home plate. They bounced up and down together in wild celebration.

"All right!"

"Nice hit, Jake!"

"We're number one!"

As he ran in from the field, Jake saw Adam, still wearing his batting helmet, bouncing and shouting in the middle of the team.

Finally, Jake thought, *I'm the hero.*

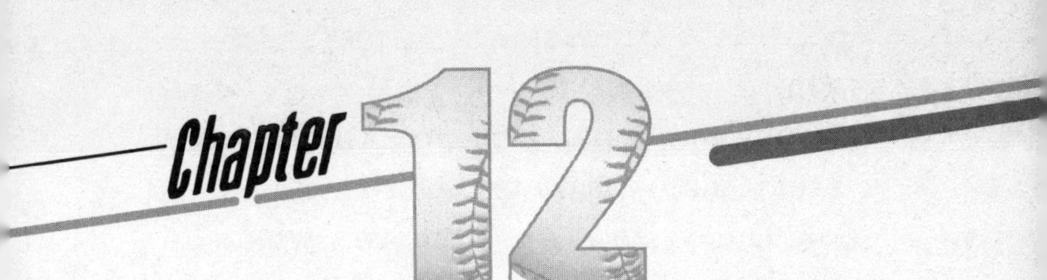

How'd you like that burger?" Jake's father asked.

"Great!" Jake said as he pushed away from the table.

"Do you have much homework?" his dad asked.

Jake shook his head. "Not really. Hey, did you ever figure out the season stats?"

"Yes." Mr. Daley paused and eyed his son. "But Coach Sanders doesn't like to show the stats to the players, remember?"

"Come on, Dad. The season's over. All we have left is the championship game against the Dodgers."

"Only?"

"You know what I mean. And anyway, you told Adam *his* stats the other night."

Mr. Daley stood up. "Tell you what. I'll print the stats off my computer. You clear the table and clean up the kitchen."

A few minutes later, Jake and his father sat on the sofa in the living room and studied the neat columns of numbers on the page.

Player	Abs	R	H	HRs	RBI	BA
Chris M.	45	15	16	0	7	.356
Jake D.	47	17	18	0	8	.383
Adam H.	42	15	24	5	24	.571
Isaiah S.	39	11	12	2	13	.308
Evan S.	41	6	12	1	8	.293
Hannah R.	35	9	14	0	10	.400
Khalil W.	32	3	9	0	3	.281
Michael R.	29	5	9	0	6	.310
Kyle K.	28	2	6	0	2	.214
Ryan D.	15	1	2	0	1	.133

Abs = At Bats
R = Runs scored
H = Hits
HRs = Home Runs
RBI = Runs Batted In
BA = Batting Average

“Wow, look at Adam,” Jake said, pointing. “He hit .571 with five home runs....” He shook his head. “I thought I was going to be the big star on the Red Sox this year. I wasn’t even close.”

“You did pretty well too,” Mr. Daley said. “You hit .383 and scored seventeen runs. And look at the numbers for Isaiah, Evan, Hannah, Chris, and Michael. Everybody helped.”

“How about Ryan?” Jake asked.

Mr. Daley smiled. “Well, he’s good in the clubhouse.”

Jake studied the statistics in silence. “Yeah, everyone did well,” he said finally. “But if we didn’t have Adam, we’d be sunk.”

“And if Adam didn’t have you guys, *he’d* be sunk,” Mr. Daley said, tapping the sheet. “Baseball is a team game. Nobody wins games by himself.”

“Adam does.”

Mr. Daley pointed to the family room. “Get me *The Baseball Encyclopedia,”* he said.

Jake got the big, heavy book and handed it, with two hands, to his father.

"Name a great baseball player," Mr. Daley said.

"Babe Ruth."

"Okay, Babe Ruth...Babe Ruth..." Jake's dad flipped through the pages. "Babe Ruth in 1927 played for the New York Yankees who won 110 games and lost only 44." He skimmed his finger across the page. "The Babe hit .356 with 60 home runs and 164 runs batted in."

"Wow!" Jake said, leaning over his father's shoulder. "He was a one-man team."

"Hardly. Look at his teammate Lou Gehrig's stats for the same year."

Jake stared at the numbers. "He hit .373 with 47 homers and 175 runs batted in."

"And the Yankees also had a second baseman named Tony Lazzeri who hit over .300 and drove in 102 runs," Mr. Daley said. "It's the same in any team sport. Name a great basketball player."

"Michael Jordan."

"Jordan never won an NBA title without Scottie Pippen," Mr. Daley said. He patted the book. "Okay, let's get back to baseball. Name another famous baseball player."

"Derek Jeter," Jake said, getting into the game.

"You're only naming Yankees?" Mr. Daley teased. "Okay, the Yankees won 116 games in 1998, but they were loaded."

"Who'd they have?"

"They had Bernie Williams and Jorge Posada. Jeter won some of those 116 games, but he didn't win them all by himself."

Just then the doorbell rang. Mr. Daley looked at his watch. "Who could that be?" he asked.

"Hey, Bernie Williams hit .339 with 26 homers that year," Jake said, still looking at *The Baseball Encyclopedia*.

Mr. Daley got up and opened the door. It was Adam's mom. "I hope I'm not disturbing your dinner. But I really had to talk to you and your wife."

"Of course," Mr. Daley said. "Please come in. But I'm sorry, my wife isn't here right now. She's at a Girl Scout meeting with Ivy."

Mrs. Hull walked in, brushing her hair

away from her face. She looked as if she'd just run a race.

"Well, maybe I can talk to you, then," Mrs. Hull said, sitting down on the couch.

"Jake, don't you have some homework?" Mr. Daley hinted to his son.

"That's all right," Mrs. Hull said, holding up a hand. "What I want to talk about involves Adam and Jake."

Jake rested the baseball book on his lap. Mrs. Hull leaned forward to the edge of the couch. "I might be moving to Los Angeles," she announced.

Mr. Daley looked surprised. "Really?" he asked. "When?"

"Soon. I have a final interview with a company the day after tomorrow," she said. "If I get the job, I would start right away. So while I'm out there, I'm planning to look for a place to live."

"What about your boys?" Mr. Daley asked.

"If I get the job, they'll move to Los Angeles with me," she said.

"What about the championship game? It's Saturday." Jake blurted out.

Mrs. Hull smiled uncomfortably. "Adam doesn't want to miss the game either. His father is away on business." She took a deep breath and turned to Mr. Daley. "Your whole family has been so good to Adam, having him over so much—"

"Adam's an easy kid," Mr. Daley interrupted. Jake didn't say anything.

"Well, thanks." Mrs. Hull smiled. "But I'd like to ask one more favor."

"Sure," Mr. Daley said.

"I'm wondering if Adam could stay here with you for a week or so? That way I could get this job thing settled and Adam wouldn't have to miss the big game."

"What about Chad?"

"He's staying with the Slaters."

Jake looked back and forth between his father and Mrs. Hull. He didn't know what to think. He wanted Adam to play in the big game. And he wanted to help Adam. After all, it couldn't be easy to have your mom and dad get divorced, move to a new town, and then have to move again to another place far away. But part of him wanted to show everyone that the Red Sox could win the championship without Adam.

Jake was tired of everyone making such a big deal out of Adam. It was as if he had taken over the team.

"I know it's a lot to ask," Mrs. Hull continued. "But could you take him just one more time?" She glanced at Jake. "It would really help Adam a lot."

Chapter 13

"You'll be staying with me in my room," Jake told Adam. He opened the bedroom door. "You can throw your stuff in here."

Adam tossed his suitcase on one of the beds. "Hey, I'll be like your big brother for a week," he said. He looked around at the framed sports posters on the walls.

"Wait a minute," Jake protested. "I'm older than you."

Adam grinned. "I said bigger, not older."

"You're not *that* much bigger," Jake said.

"Let's see," Adam said, grabbing a pencil from the desk. "Stand up against the doorframe." Jake stood against the edge. Adam leveled the pencil along the top of his head and made a small mark on the wood.

"Now me," Adam said. The boys switched places. Sure enough, Adam was at least two inches taller than Jake. "See, I'm the big brother," Adam said as he continued to look around the room. "Hey, you've got our schedule up here." He pointed at the wall next to Jake's desk. Adam studied the schedule.

RED SOX SCHEDULE

Date	**Opponent**	**Time**	
Sat. April 18	Braves	2 pm	W 6-4
Wed. April 22	Royals	6:30 pm	W 3-1
Sat. April 25	Yankees	noon	W 10-1
Tues. April 28	Dodgers	6:30 pm	L 3-0
Sat. May 2	Reds	4 pm	W 8-6
Thurs. May 7	Giants	6:30 pm	W 14-7
Sat. May 9	Tigers	10 am	W 4-2
Tues. May 12	Braves	6:30 pm	W 7-3
Sat. May 16	Royals	noon	W 5-4
Sat. May 23	Yankees	2 pm	W 8-0
Wed. May 27	Dodgers	6:30 pm	W 2-1
Sat. May 30	Reds	4 pm	L 5-3
Wed. June 3	Giants	6:30 pm	W 12-2
Sat. June 6	Tigers	noon	W 3-2
Sat. June 13	Championship Game		

"Twelve wins, two losses. That's pretty good," he said.

"Good enough to make the championship game," Jake said.

"Who are we playing again?" Adam asked. He flopped back on the bed, reached down to grab a football from the floor, and began tossing it toward the ceiling.

"The Dodgers." Jake grabbed the football out of the air. "They're really good."

"We'll beat them anyway," Adam said. He popped up from the bed. "Let's play that Outs game in your backyard."

"I don't know," Jake said, remembering how he'd lost the last game. "I don't feel like—"

"Come on," Adam said. "Don't you want to get your championship back?"

"Okay," Jake said, rising to the challenge. "Grab your glove."

The boys raced down the stairs. "Where are you two going?" Mr. Daley called from his downstairs office.

"The yard," Jake called back. "We're going to throw the ball around." He and

Adam burst out the back door. The screen door whacked shut.

"I'm up first," Adam said.

"Okay, I'm home team," Jake said.

"I have an advantage this time." Adam held up his glove. "I've got my own mitt." Then he looked at the side of the house and fixed his eyes on Jake's secret home-run spot. "And I know all your tricks now," he added with a smile. "You ready?"

Jake walked back to his fielding position. "Okay, you're up," he said. He could already sense defeat.

Adam looked at Jake and then at the house again. He pivoted and threw hard at Jake's secret spot.

Whack! The ball smacked against the house and rocketed through the air. Adam threw a triumphant fist toward the sky, certain it was a home run.

Jake drifted back until he was just inches from the fence. He looked up and saw the ball falling right toward him. He jumped as high as he could, reaching up...up...up. At the top of his leap, he snagged the ball in the tip of his glove.

Adam's fist dropped to his side. "What?" he cried out.

Jake proudly tossed the ball back to his friend. Adam caught it and smiled. "That was a pretty good catch," he said. "Hope you make some as good as that on Saturday."

Come on, guys, time to wake up," Mr. Daley said as he knocked on the door and walked into Jake's bedroom. He pulled up the window shade and the Saturday morning sunshine poured in.

"It's eight o'clock," Jake's dad said in a cheery voice. "Game starts at ten. You guys need to eat a good breakfast and get to the field by 9:30 to warm up."

He slapped Adam on the back. "Especially you, Adam. You're pitching."

Jake pushed himself up in his bed. "Is anybody else going to pitch?" he asked.

"I don't know. It's the championship game, so Coach Sanders will only bring in new pitchers if Adam needs help or he runs out of pitches." Mr. Daley picked some dirty clothes off the floor and dropped them in the hamper. "The rule is that no pitcher can throw more than seventy-five pitches in a game."

"When did they come up with that rule?" Adam asked.

"It's been the rule all year," Mr. Daley explained. "But it didn't matter because Coach Sanders usually only lets kids pitch three innings anyway. Today is different. It's the championship game. So let's get going."

Jake rolled over in bed after his father left. Adam got up right away and used the bathroom first.

Lying in bed, Jake thought back over the past week. It had actually been kind of fun having Adam around. He loved to play games with him and talk about sports. A few times Jake had tried to talk to Adam about his move to Los Angeles, but Adam hadn't said that much.

One thing was different now, though.

After being with Adam so much, Jake could see that he was more like a regular kid, not a big sports star.

"Your turn," Adam said as he walked back into the bedroom and flopped face-first onto his bed. "I'm so tired," he wailed. "I want to go back to sleep."

Jake grabbed Adam by his ankles and started pulling him across the bed. "You gotta get up," he said. "You're pitching, remember?"

"No, no, let me sleep." Adam laughed, holding on to the bedpost. "You guys can win without me."

"Maybe," Jake said. "But it'll be a lot easier to win *with* you."

Later that morning, Jake stood at shortstop, toeing the infield dirt with his cleats. It's a good thing he'd gotten Adam out of bed. There was no way they could win this game without him.

The Red Sox led the Dodgers 1–0 in the bottom of the fourth inning. Adam had driven in the only run and had pitched a two-hit shutout for almost four innings.

Adam wound up and fired another fastball. The Dodgers batter swung hard but missed. "Strike three!" The inning was over.

The Red Sox ran back to their bench to start the fifth inning.

"Evan, Hannah, Khalil, then Michael," Mr. Daley called out. "Come on, we need some more runs."

Jake put his glove on the bench and walked over to his father. "How many pitches has Adam thrown?" he asked.

"Fifty-six," his father said, without checking his laptop.

Only nineteen pitches left and two innings to go, Jake thought.

"It's going to be close," Mr. Daley said.

The Red Sox didn't score in the top of the inning. "Come on, 1-2-3 inning," Jake yelled as he ran back out to shortstop. He really meant it. The Red Sox needed outs…fast.

The leadoff Dodgers batter let the first pitch fly by. Ball one.

"Make him put it over," the Dodgers third-base coach called, clapping his hands.

Adam tugged at his hat as he stood on

the mound. Then he focused on Evan, who was crouched behind home plate, flashing finger signals.

Adam nodded, and went into his windup. The second pitch cut the heart of the plate. Strike one!

The Dodgers batter topped a slow grounder to shortstop on the next pitch. Jake rushed in, scooped up the ball, and, still leaning forward, made a hard, side-armed throw to first base.

"You're out!" the umpire at first called.

"All right!" Adam yelled from the mound. "Great play, Jake."

Jake returned to shortstop smiling. He had saved a hit and a base runner. But maybe even more importantly, his play had saved Adam some pitches.

Adam threw two quick strikes by the second Dodgers hitter. The third pitch just missed the outside corner. One ball, two strikes.

"Come on, Adam!" Jake cheered. "Go right after him." *Six pitches already,* he thought. *Adam only has thirteen left.*

The Dodgers batter sliced the next pitch foul. Then he topped a squibbler toward third base that drifted foul in front of the bag.

"Good at bat," the third base coach said. "Hang in there."

The batter popped the next pitch in foul territory, down the left-field line. The third baseman, left fielder, and Jake raced over. Jake called it as he hurried to the ball, but he ran out of room, bumping into the side fence. The ball fell on the other side of the fence just a few feet beyond Jake's outstretched glove. Jake smacked his glove against the wooden fence.

The batter fouled off two more pitches. Jake pounded his glove. "Come on, Adam. One more strike."

Adam threw a changeup.

Swinging off balance, the batter lifted a weak pop fly just beyond third base.

"I've got it!" Jake called just before the ball settled into his glove for the second out. "Two away," he said, signaling the outfield after he tossed the ball back to Adam.

Adam threw two pitches wide of the mark to the next Dodgers batter. Two balls, no strikes. He battled back with two fastballs that caught the edge of the plate. Two balls, two strikes.

Adam went into his windup. From shortstop, Jake could see that he was putting something extra on this fastball. The pitch sizzled toward the plate. The Dodgers batter swung and missed.

Strike three!

Jake's mind filled with calculations as he ran off the field. No runs, no hits, no errors. The Red Sox had gotten their 1-2-3 inning. But Adam had thrown 17 pitches during the fifth inning. Jake made one final calculation as he dropped onto the Red Sox bench for the final inning. Fifty-six plus 17 equaled 73. Adam had thrown 73 pitches. That meant he had only two pitches left.

Even Adam couldn't win this game all by himself.

Jake looked down the Red Sox bench. Coach Sanders and Jake's dad were checking the game stats and talking.

Ryan sat down between Jake and Adam. "We've got it made," he said, slapping Adam on the shoulder. "You're pitching great."

"Shut up!" Jake said, slamming his glove into the dugout dirt.

"What's with you?" Ryan asked.

"Adam has only two more pitches left," Jake snapped.

"Are you kidding?" Ryan said. "He can throw a hundred more pitches."

"Sorry, Ryan," Adam said softly. "Jake's right."

"What?"

"It's the seventy-five-pitch rule, remember?" Jake explained. "A pitcher can't throw more than seventy-five pitches in a game. Adam's already thrown seventy-three."

Jake stood up and began to pace. "Even Adam can't get three outs on two pitches."

"All right, everybody, listen up," Coach Sanders called. He motioned for the team to gather around him. "Great game, Adam, but I have to take you out. You're almost at the seventy-five-pitch limit."

The circle of Red Sox stirred at the news. The coach kept talking. "Isaiah, warm up. You'll go in for Adam. Throw strikes, no free passes. Adam, you go to shortstop. Jake, you're at second. Michael, switch to third base."

No one on the Red Sox bench said a word. They knew what they had to do.

Coach Sanders clapped his hands. "We're only up by one run," he said, holding up one finger. "Let's get some more."

But the Red Sox could only get one hit in the top of the sixth inning and no runs.

They were still 1–0 when the team ran out to their positions.

"Come on, Isaiah," Jake called from second base. "Nothing but strikes. Let's have a 1-2-3 inning."

Isaiah got the first out as the leadoff batter popped up to first base. The second batter pulled a hard line drive down the left-field line and cruised into second base with a double. Runner on second, one out. The Red Sox one-run lead was hanging by a thread.

Isaiah reared back and got a little extra on his fastball to strike out the next Dodgers batter. "Two outs," Jake called to the outfielders. Then he turned back to the infield, pounded his glove, and pleaded, "Just one more, Isaiah."

The next batter chopped a hard, high hopper over Isaiah's head. Jake and Adam ran toward second base, trying desperately to cut off the bouncing ball. But it skipped between the two infielders and into the outfield as the Dodgers runner on second raced home.

Standing helplessly at second base, Jake and Adam looked at each other without saying a word. The score was tied.

The inning ended as Hannah made a running catch of a fly ball in left field. The crowd stood and cheered as the Red Sox came running in and the Dodgers went back out on the field. The championship game was going into extra innings.

Neither team could push across a run in the seventh or eighth innings. Chris made a diving catch in center field and Michael snagged a screaming line drive at third base to keep the Dodgers scoreless.

"Jake, Adam, Isaiah, Evan!" Mr. Daley called out as the Red Sox got ready to bat in the top of the ninth. "Let's get some hits."

Jake gave his team hope as he smacked a clean single to center to start the inning.

"Come on, Adam!" Jake cheered, standing on first base and clapping his hands. "Knock it out of the park."

Adam swung hard and lifted a pitch high into left field.

"All right!" Jake yelled, punching the air as he jogged to second base.

But the Dodgers left fielder drifted back and caught the ball a foot from the fence. Adam kicked the dirt. Jake scrambled back to first base. One out.

"Come on, Isaiah!" Jake yelled. "We need a hit."

Isaiah came through, slashing a single to right center field. Jake was off at the crack of the bat, sprinting around second base and sliding into third. The Red Sox had runners at the corners, first and third, with one out.

Coach Sanders stepped away from the Red Sox bench and looked directly at Jake. "Make sure a line drive gets past the infield. Be ready to run," the coach said.

Evan got into his batter's stance and snuck a quick glance at Coach Sanders. The coach wiped his right hand across his chest and grabbed the bill of his cap with both hands.

The bunt signal, Jake thought, standing on third. *Coach is going to try to win the game on a squeeze play!*

Jake checked the Dodgers third baseman. He was standing several steps behind third base. *This just might work,* Jake told himself.

The Dodgers pitcher wound up and threw hard. At the last moment, Evan squared around and knocked a slow roller down the third-base line.

Jake was off, sprinting toward home.

"First base, first base!" the Dodgers pitcher called as the third baseman fielded the ball. The Dodgers didn't even try to get Jake at home. Instead, they threw the ball to first.

The squeeze play had worked!

"Great job, Evan! Way to go!" Coach Sanders was grinning from ear to ear. The Red Sox were ahead, 2–1!

The team flew onto the field after the third out, filling the infield with chatter.

"One-two-three inning."

"Nothing but strikes."

"Tight defense."

The leadoff hitter for the Dodgers rapped a hard grounder to shortstop. Adam fielded it cleanly, but threw low to first base. Khalil, the Red Sox first baseman, scooped the throw out of the dirt. One out.

Everybody is making plays, Jake thought as Khalil tossed the ball back to Sam, the new Red Sox pitcher. *Chris, Hannah, Michael, Khalil. The whole team.*

Two straight singles wiped the smile off Jake's face. Suddenly the Dodgers had runners at first and third, with one out. Coach Sanders called time-out and walked slowly to the pitcher's mound. The Red Sox infielders gathered around.

"All right, here's what we'll do," he said as he eyed the base runner. "Isaiah and Khalil play in front of the bags at first and third. I don't want them trying a bunt like we did."

"What about Jake and me?" Adam asked.

"You guys play back. If the ball comes to you, try for the double play, just like we practiced."

Coach Sanders put his hand on Sam's pitching shoulder. "Try to keep your pitches low in the strike zone," he instructed. "Maybe we can get a ground ball."

Sam threw a low fastball. The Dodgers hitter smashed a hard grounder up the middle. Adam quickly raced over, snapped the ball up in his glove, and flipped the ball to second base.

Jake was ready. He caught Adam's throw, touched second base with his left foot, and, just like in practice, pivoted toward first base. Jake knew his throw would have to be hard and quick. He gave it all he had. The ball smacked into Khalil's mitt just before the runner flashed across the bag.

"You're out!" the umpire called.

A double play. The game was over. The Red Sox had won the championship, 2–1!

A wild celebration erupted in the middle of the field. All the Red Sox raced to the pitcher's mound, jumping up and down and throwing their hats and mitts into the air. Jake saw Adam laughing and smiling with all of their teammates, just like before.

Then it suddenly hit him: This might be Adam's last game for the Red Sox.

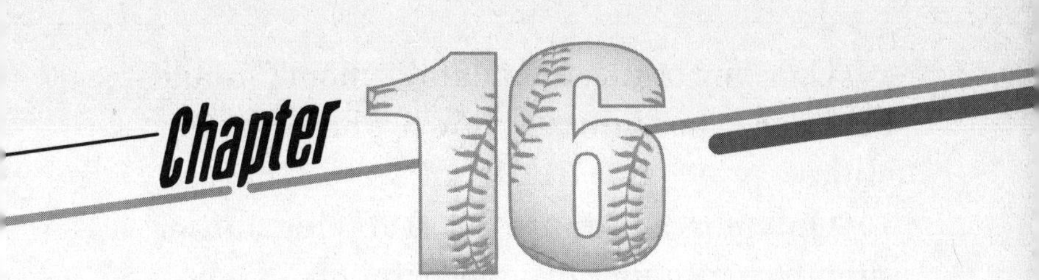

Chapter 16

Jake sat on the edge of his bed. The other bed was stripped of its blanket and sheets. The mattress was bare.

Earlier in the day, Jake's father had taken Adam back home on his way to a meeting. Now Jake's house seemed empty and quiet without his "big brother." He looked over at the Red Sox schedule where Adam had penciled in the team's 2–1 win in nine innings in the championship game. Then he heard a car pull into the driveway and a car door shut. Jake bounced off the bed and ran downstairs. His father came through the front door and dropped his car keys on the hall table.

"Did you talk to Adam's mom?" Jake asked as he jumped down the last few stairs.

"Only for a minute or two," his father said. "I really just dropped him off."

"Well, did she get the job?" Jake asked. "Does Adam have to move?"

Mr. Daley shrugged. "I'm not sure. She didn't say. My guess is that she wants to talk to Adam and Chad first."

Jake walked over to the living room window and gazed out. His father sat down in the living room and looked at Jake. "I guess if Adam moves," he said, "you'll probably play shortstop all the time in the fall."

"I know," Jake said, still looking out the window. "But we won't be as good without Adam."

Mr. Daley nodded silently. Jake turned and looked back at his dad. "You know, I wouldn't mind being Lou Gehrig," he said.

"Or Bernie Williams." His father smiled.

"Or Scottie Pippen," Jake said.

"We'll see," Mr. Daley said.

Jake grabbed his glove and a tennis ball

and went into the backyard. He threw the ball hard against the back of the house and fielded grounder after grounder.

"Nice play," a familiar voice called. "For a second baseman."

Jake turned and saw Adam standing at the corner of the yard as he had so many times before. "Did your mom get the job?" The words almost jumped out of Jake's mouth.

"Yep," Adam said.

Jake felt as if someone had punched him in the stomach. So it was true. Adam was leaving. "When do you move?" he asked.

"We're not gonna move," Adam said. He held his hands open and motioned for the ball.

"Not gonna move?" Jake repeated as he tossed the ball to his friend. "I thought you said that your mom got the job."

"She did." Adam tossed the ball back and forth between his hands. "But when she told her boss at her job here, they decided to give her a big raise..." Adam paused and tossed the ball into the air.

"Yeah, so what happened?" Jake asked.

Adam smiled. "So my mom decided to stay. She said it was important for me and Chad to be close to our dad. Besides, I'm already on a team and everything."

The boys started to throw the ball back and forth as they talked. "That's great," Jake said. "We'll be on the Red Sox together again next season."

"Yeah," Adam said. "We'll turn a million double plays." He caught the ball and turned toward the back of the house. "And we can keep playing for the Outs championship." He held up the ball and said, "I'm up first."

Jake scrambled back to his fielding position.

Thwack! The tennis ball hit the house and cruised high in the summer sky. Jake raced back to the fence and leaped higher than he had ever leaped. But this time the ball sailed over his outstretched glove and over the fence. "I almost had it!" Jake shouted.

"Better watch out," Adam said. "I'm

gonna be the Babe Ruth of Outs from now on."

Jake thought back on the Red Sox season, what his father had said about the importance of teammates, and all he and Adam had been through together. "Okay," he said. "I'll be Lou Gehrig."

"Who's that?" Adam asked.

Jake laughed. "I'll tell you later. Come on," he said. "Let's keep playing."

The Real Story

Jake's father was right. In team sports there is no such thing as a one-man or one-woman team. Even the greatest players need help. They need good teammates.

In baseball, many people say that Babe Ruth was the greatest player ever. Ruth won six World Series championships during his career with the Boston Red Sox and the New York Yankees. But even the Great Bambino, as Ruth was called, didn't win those championships by himself.

Lou Gehrig was the Yanks' first baseman and cleanup hitter for three of the four championship Yankee teams Ruth played on. Gehrig was called the Iron Horse because he appeared in 2,130 consecutive games during the 1920s and 30s and, like Ruth, was one of baseball's greatest players. Gehrig had a career batting average of .340, with a walloping 493 home runs.

Gehrig was at his very best during the 1932 World Series. He batted .529 with three home runs and eight runs batted in (RBI) to lead the Yankees in a four-game sweep of the Chicago Cubs.

After Ruth retired, Gehrig helped the Yankees win three more World Series (1936, 1937, and 1938). But Gehrig didn't win those championships alone. A marvelous young center fielder named Joe DiMaggio began playing with the Yankees in 1936. Joltin' Joe batted over .320 and belted more than 125 RBIs in each of his first three seasons.

Michael Jordan won ten National Basketball Association (NBA) scoring titles and six NBA titles while playing with the Chicago Bulls. But Jordan never won an NBA championship without Scottie Pippen.

Pippen was not well known at first because he had attended a small college (the University of Central Arkansas). But in the pros, Pippen proved that he was a versatile forward who could score, rebound, and pass with the best of them. For example, in the Bulls first championship season (1991), Pippen averaged more than 21 points per game during the playoffs while grabbing almost nine rebounds and dealing out almost six assists. The Bulls also had other terrific players to help Jordan, such as forwards Horace Grant and Tony Kukoc, as well as guards Steve Kerr and B. J. Armstrong.

In fact, Jordan's Chicago teammates were so good that when he took time off to play baseball, the Bulls still won 55 games without him. That was only two games fewer than they had won the year before *with* Jordan.

A star player's teammates are important in all team sports. Many people believe that Joe Montana was the best quarterback in the history of professional football. Montana led the San Francisco 49ers to four Super

Bowl championships and was named the Most Valuable Player (MVP) in three of those Super Bowls. But any quarterback needs receivers who can get open and catch their passes.

In fact, Montana had one of the best of those receivers for many of his years with the 49ers. Jerry Rice owns the records for most career receptions, touchdowns, and yards gained from catching passes in the history of the National Football League. For years, Rice and Montana made a great team for the 49ers.

And no quarterback, not even a great one like Montana, can complete passes and throw touchdowns unless he has time to set up and find his receivers. He has to have great offensive linemen blocking for him too.

Soccer star Mia Hamm scored more goals (158) in international competition than any other player, male or female. Hamm's U.S. national teams won the World Cup in 1991 and 1999 and the Olympic gold medals in 1996 and 2004.

But again, Hamm was not alone out there on the field. No scorer in international soccer can dribble through an entire team. She needs teammates who can get her the ball when she has a chance to score. Hamm played with such American soccer standouts as Michelle Akers, Brandi Chastain, Kristine Lilly, and Abby Wambach. Hamm herself insisted that Lilly was the best all-around player on the legendary 1999 World Cup team.

In baseball or any other team sport, every player must do his or her best to help the team win. Teams need the Babe Ruths and the Michael Jordans. But as Jake learned, they also need the Lou Gehrigs and the Scottie Pippens.

Special thanks to Samantha Frank
for her help in typing the original manuscript.

About the Author

FRED BOWEN was a Little Leaguer who loved to read. Now he is the author of many action-packed books of sports fiction. He has also written a weekly sports column for kids in the *Washington Post* since 2000.

For thirteen years, Fred coached kids' baseball and basketball teams. Some of his stories spring directly from his coaching experience and his sports-happy childhood in Marblehead, Massachusetts.

Fred holds a degree in history from the University of Pennsylvania and a law degree from George Washington University. He was a lawyer for many years before retiring to become a full-time children's author. Bowen has been a guest author at schools and conferences across the country, as well as the Smithsonian Institute in Washington, D.C., and The Baseball Hall of Fame.

Fred lives in Silver Spring, Maryland, with his wife Peggy Jackson. Their son is a college baseball coach and their daughter is a graduate student in Colorado studying to become a teacher.

For more information
check out the author's website at
www.fredbowen.com.

Real Hoops

PB: $5.95 / 978-1-56145-566-9

Hud can run, pass, and shoot at top speed. But he's not much of a team player. Can Ben convince Hud to leave his dazzling—but one-man—style back on the asphalt?

Quarterback Season

PB: $5.95 / 978-1-56145-594-2

Matt expects to be the starting quarterback. But after a few practices watching Devro, a talented seventh grade he's starting to get nervous. To make matters worse, his English teacher is on his case about a new class assignment: a journal.

Go for the Goal!

PB: $5.95 / 978-1-56145-632-1

Josh and his talented travel league soccer teammates are having trouble coming together as a successful team—until he convinces them to try team-building exercises.

Perfect Game

PB: $5.95 / 978-1-56145-594-2

HC: $13.95 / 978-1-56145-701-4

Isaac is determined to pitch a perfect game—no hits, n runs, no walks, and no errors. He gets close a couple o times, but when things go wrong he can't get his head back in the game. Then Isaac meets an interesting Unified Sports basketball player who shows him a whol new way to think about *perfect*.

Double Reverse

PB: $5.95 / 978-1-56145-807-3

HC: $13.95 / 978-1-56145-814-1

The season starts off badly, and things get even worse when the Panthers quarterback is injured. Jesse know the playbook by heart, but he feels that he's too small f the role. He just doesn't look the part. Can he play against type and help the Panthers become a winning team?

Check out **www.SportsStorySeries.com** for more info.

Want more?

All-Star Sports Story *Series*

All-Star Sports Story series

T. J.'s Secret Pitch

PB: $5.95 / 978-1-56145-504-1

T. J.'s pitches just don't pack the power they need to strike out the batters, but the story of 1940s baseball hero Rip Sewell and his legendary eephus pitch may help him find a solution.

The Golden Glove

PB: $5.95 / 978-1-56145-505-8

Without his lucky glove, Jamie doesn't believe in his ability to lead his baseball team to victory. How will he learn that faith in oneself is the most important equipment for any game?

The Kid Coach

PB: $5.95 / 978-1-56145-506-5

Scott and his teammates can't find an adult to coach their team, so they must find a leader among themselves.

Playoff Dreams

PB: $5.95 / 978-1-56145-507-2

Brendan is one of the best players in the league, but no matter how hard he tries, he can't make his team win.

Winners Take All

PB: $5.95 / 978-1-56145-512-6

Kyle makes a poor decision to cheat in a big game. Someone discovers the truth and threatens to reveal it. What can Kyle do now?

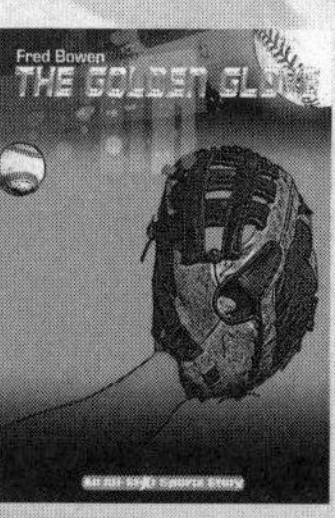

All-Star Sports Story Series

All-Star Sports Story *Series*

Full Court Fever

PB: $5.95 / 978-1-56145-508-9

The Falcons have the skill but not the height to win their games. Will the full-court zone press be the solution to their problem?

Off the Rim

PB: $5.95 / 978-1-56145-509-6

Hoping to be more than a benchwarmer, Chris learns that defense is just as important as offense.

The Final Cut

PB: $5.95 / 978-1-56145-510-2

Four friends realize that they may not all make the team and that the tryouts are a test—not only of their athletic skills, but also of their friendship.

On the Line

PB: $5.95 / 978-1-56145-511-9

Marcus is the highest scorer and the best rebounder, but he's not so great at free throws—until the school custodian helps him overcome his fear of failure.

Check out **www.SportsStorySeries.com** for more info.